Seven Deadly Sins

Seven Deadly Sins

Seven Deadly Sins

Seven Deadly Sins

Seven Deadly Sins

Table of Contents

Chapter One

DEATH.

IT WAS SOMETHING UNAVOIDABLE. That should have been true. It used to be true, at least, fifty years ago. But now…

Just thinking about it was enough to make Slater Frost chuckle. It wasn't a happy laugh, but a bitter one. He stood outside of his house, in the light of day, and couldn't even feel the way that the sun hit his skin. It might not even touch him now, though part of his flesh still glowed with alabaster delight. It felt, recently, as if there was something wrong with the nerve endings.

Touch was a little less. Feelings were a little less. Water had to be either frozen or burning for him to feel it on his hands, and his tongue seemed numb to everything but the absolute strongest of flavors. And yet, there he stood, alive, even if not well, thinking about death on a possibly bright, possibly sunny, afternoon.

Slater was an elderly man, with thinning gray hair and deep lines on his face. Each day, he looked at the world in front of him — at the changes in it. The changes that had taken place seemingly both quickly and slowly, all at the same time — and he found that looking away was too difficult.

No.

Not just difficult. It was almost impossible. This world was here, and that terrified him.

Winds carrying the smell of death itself breezed through him, ruffling his exquisite-looking clothes. He could smell it, smell the sheer rot that was in the wind itself. He could smell everything, from the way the decay and destruction moved in the air to the smell of blood.

It was putrid and sour, the sort of tang that made his mouth water. Not too long ago, the smell would have made his stomach heave, too. But funny, wasn't it, that he could get used to even this? To the way that fetid blood curdled the air, to the way that a dying society blossomed into scents like the world's most ill-regarded bouquet?

There was so much blood. It seemed to be everywhere. It seemed to be in everything. Slater pulled in a deep breath, forcing that putrid air into his lungs until it made his chest ache. Then, he straightened out the front of his shirt, smoothing his hands down over the white cloth, crooked fingers catching on the buttons of it.

"Come on," he told himself, and proceeded to not take a single step.

Around him was the end of all things.

"Walk," he told himself, petulantly.

Slowly, his feet began to move. He leaned upon a polished cane, which had the head of a lion for the top. A large pearl was caught in the lion's mouth. It had been beautiful at the time, fitting even.

Once, Slater had thought himself to be exactly the same as that lion. He was a king in his youth. A man ready to take on the world. This whole city had been brimming with people just like him, determined to make something of themselves. But now... now everything was different.

He could see how the years had ravaged everyone, and looking at it, all he was reminded of was an article he had read. It must have been fifty years ago that he'd picked up that newspaper, but the words written within still echoed about in his skull.

Death is a concept that has plagued life itself since its beginning. Everyone knows that what starts must come to an end, and what ends must begin again. History repeats itself, as one says, only one cannot tell how often it will repeat itself.

Slater couldn't remember anything else about that article, not anymore. His memory wasn't like it used to be. But that line, it stood out to him. He could hear it in his sleep some nights. Could hear the words as they bounced around in the empty house, somehow both a comfort and a mocking joke.

He had been afraid of it. He had been afraid of death, of going into a slumber so deep that he would never wake up again. He had been afraid of missing out on the world, on how this world operated, on how this world made the beauty of it appear out in the open by simply existing with each other.

That might not have seemed so unusual, so awful. Many people were afraid of death. The concept of forever going into a true unknown was enough to bring grown men to their knees. It was part of why some people prayed — although religion was hard to come by these days. People had turned to other means of getting help and comfort.

Slater was not alone in his fear of death. Far from it. However, he was one of the few who had been able to find an alternate route and had taken it.

He didn't want to go away; he didn't want to know what would happen to himself. He didn't want to know what he would do if he didn't get a chance to see his family grow, to see his successes grow, to see what he managed to do in the world.

He was a smart man, after all. Carnelian City, in its youth, had been kind to him. His wife had passed away years before — Cordelia, a lovely woman who had taken Slater's heart when she died — but he had a son, and he had grandchildren, and they meant a great deal to him. They lived in Carnelian City, too. They were all flourishing within the warmth of the city's seemingly endless generosity. To leave that behind, in death, seemed like a sin.

But that wasn't it.

Oh, Slater would tell you, "I don't want to die because I need to see how my family fares. I need to make sure that they're all taken care of, you know?"

His son, Clayton, would shake his head, "You don't need to worry about us, Dad. We're going to be just fine. Did you see what Arlyne built the other day? He'll be an inventor someday, I'm sure. They're going to want him at Cryo Corps."

And Slater, a coward, would quickly change the subject from death to the future of his grandson, asking, "Is that such a good idea, though?"

The conversation was always the same. Clayton would roll his eyes and say, "It's all he's ever wanted. And they pay well. He can create literally anything in their labs, even things once thought impossible."

Bitter, Slater would go on a rant — Cryo Corps was not stationed in Carnelian City. They were out of bounds, nearly three hours to the north, in Hydroark. And yes, they would give Arlyne the supplies to build and create anything in the world, anything that his heart might desire, anything to save the world — but then they would own it, too, would take it, and claim it as their own.

Generosity died outside of Carnelian City.

It was a good excuse… but it wasn't the truth.

No, Slater was afraid of dying for something much worse. He was afraid that if he died, he would just be forgotten. A name, written on a stone, and nothing else. Arlyne, that boy had a future. He had something going for him. A real chance to change things. Only sixteen, and already the Cryo Corps was watching him.

But Slater?

He'd done next to nothing with his life. Built a family. A home. A decent business, but only by the standards of Carnelian City. He had friends, sure, but none so close that they would write poetry about him for years after he was gone.

Slater didn't just face uncertainty when he died.

He faced obscurity.

That was terrifying.

He didn't want that. He didn't want people to forget about him; he didn't want people to completely forget about him and never remember him ever again. He didn't want people to forget who he was, what he had done, why he existed. And that was why he also had done it. He had bought one of the revolutionary pills.

And oh — there's a story there. A tale about what had happened in those fifty years. But Slater didn't like to think about it. The glory he had sought didn't exist. Instead, the city had changed. Had twisted, broken, and fallen. And now, it was this.

And fifty long years had passed since then. Fifty years of watching how the pills had changed the world. Fifty years of watching how the life of this proud, lustrous, and bright man had turned into something that was akin to a nightmare, dark and black, unable to even comprehend how life could be as such.

It got difficult to see at times, and he had hidden. Hid and stayed away, but even hiding did not change anything. Even hiding did not assure that he would be able to escape the blanket of darkness and despair that had overtaken the world. But he survived. Even when everyone and everything was dying, he survived. He lived, and he watched. Watched as his foolishness, his stupidity, made sure he would be there until the end of time.

And oh, but the world was so empty now! There was so little left to see, even here, in Carnelian City. Or perhaps, it was especially noticeable in Carnelian City because he knew what the world used to be like.

Once, the city in front of him was beautiful. Very beautiful. It was the city of dreams, with gardens blooming in colorful flowers, streets bustling with all types and manners of vehicles, and ideas getting a chance to be reality. Carnelian City was a place where no one would ever go hungry; there were food shops on every corner, filling the air with the scent of freshly-baked sesame rolls, sweet honey cake, and fluffy buttermilk biscuits. On other streets, flower shops were thriving.

Fifty years ago, there had been a trend. Flowers in everything. Your hair, your car, your home. If you had a green thumb and a smart mind for business, then you could literally bloom into a man or woman of wealth and esteem overnight.

And it wasn't just the business side of things.

Carnelian City was special, because the people who lived and worked there were generous. There were no wastes. There was nothing that got put aside, left, forgotten, or thrown away. It was a city that took what others might discard and found a new use for them.

Sometimes, that meant giving away food at the end of the day. Other times, it meant taking what had been discarded and turning it into something new — furniture made from broken crates, blankets made from old couch cushions, clothing made from torn blankets. The people of Carnelian City were smart. They were smart, and they were kind.

That wasn't a combination that Slater had found anywhere else in the world.

In Carnelian City, everyone was kept healthy and happy.

The motto of Carnelian City was "We Thrive Together," and it was thought that if the community let each other down, then it would let itself down. It was a city that was founded on the belief that no one could make it through life on their own; they needed to rely on each other. Humanity thrived best when people were working together.

It was thought, in Carnelian at least, that no one could survive as a singularity. It took a village to raise a child; it took a city to form a future; it took people, as a whole, as a collective, to create a world that was worth living in. And all that Carnelian wanted, more than anything, was to be a town that was worth living in.

In fact, it was a priority. The city itself was built to reflect the purity of humanity. Just as the people held a white glow to them, the buildings were made to mimic that. The white stone work was accentuated with the many flowers that were sold and brightly-colored cloth banners. During the holidays, the stone would find itself covered in bright rainbow confetti. And then when the celebration was done, it wouldn't be left to one person or another to clean; it would be a group effort — another celebration of its own, as the people descended onto the streets with brooms and cloths and water, and they brought with them treats and drinks for the long hours that waited ahead.

Winter wasn't much different. The city was purer then, as the snow fell down. It was a blanket of white on top of a world of white; sometimes, you could lose yourself in it. Sit down on the ground and just let the stillness of it all swallow you. The winters were not harsh, and Carnelian City was such that no one was left to try and weather the season outside alone.

Even if you didn't have a family, there was always someone to spend it with. Community functions were a driving point behind it all. They worked together to ensure that the city was kept up with, that nothing was forgotten, that no one was overlooked. Food given away. Warm clothes mended whether you could afford it or not. People back then had never met but in passing, joining to help create a better year for each other.

Life was a struggle, but like every struggle, two hands made it better than one. When they helped people out, they would be helped out in return. That was what made Carnelian City so different. That was why people pulled together and chose to stay there, why they would travel from all over the world, choosing to put down their roots and start their families in Carnelian City! That was what had drawn Slater there, what seemed like a lifetime ago.

Cordelia had still been alive then, and she said to him one day, "I'm tired of this place. The Winding Roads don't have anything to offer us."

Their house, at the time, was in a section of land called the Winding Roads. It was popular for merchants, as the main roads wrapped around the homes, who could then earn their coin with room and board, food and sales, or other such novelties.

Cordelia had been a quilter before her hands and her eyes started to give her trouble.

Now, they just lived there with no sales to offer.

Slater said, "We make a good living, selling out that spare room of ours. People like staying with us."

"But look outside! This land is so ugly. Did you know, Wilder passed away?"

"Who?"

"He lived next door for three years," said Cordelia, as if that was proving her point. "It took someone stopping to buy from him for his loss to be noticed. Dead and rotting on that floor for a solid week, they say."

Slater had taken hold of her hand. "That won't happen to you," he'd told her. "I won't let it."

But Cordelia had made up her mind. She no longer wanted to live at the Winding Roads. She wanted to find somewhere to live where people were more compassionate, where they knew each other. And that's why they had gone to Carnelian City.

Slater had been amazed by the difference! The people here were so… different.

He remembered watching a street-baker offer a hungry homeless woman some food for her children one day, and almost three months later, he saw the same woman, who was once homeless, opening up her own shop right next door to the baker, a grocery shop, and supplying the baker with everything he needed without charging him.

That had just been one case of many. Stories like that were a dime a dozen in Carnelian City. The people there were just good. When someone needed help, others stepped up. They repaired homes and businesses after bad storms. They stepped up to help when illness took over. They didn't let anyone suffer alone. In fact, very few people were even put into a place where they needed to suffer! That's just not how it was done.

They were a family without being a family. They were friends without being friends. These people looked at the world around them, and they made the decision that they wanted it to be better. That they would do anything it took to make the world better. Safer. Happier.

That was admirable.

And so, Cordelia and Slater stayed in Carnelian City. They stayed and made a life for themselves, relishing in the companionship that the city offered.

Co-operation and content went side-by-side. It was no utopia, that's for sure. There were problems. People were fired. People got sick. But unlike other parts of the world, when a problem arrived, Carnelian City gathered together to help it recover and survive.

Maybe that's why it was so much harder to see Carnelian City fall compared to the rest of the world. Because this had been one of those few places where things were actually good. Where the people here were actually, genuinely good.

But everything was then slowly destroyed. Piece by piece, the world began to change. Those first few years, it happened so slowly that it was almost missed. Slater certainly hadn't taken notice of it back then. Maybe that was a sign. Maybe it proved that he'd always been selfish. Too concerned with his own life to see how the pills were affecting the world around him and the lives of the others who had once lived in Carnelian City.

The radiant glow of people slowly started to change as the pills came into the market. It had been gradually slow — the dimness hadn't even been noticeable at the start! But as their glow began to fade and more darkness crept into the world around them, their personalities began to change, too. There was no generosity to be found in Carnelian City anymore. There was no kindness. No constant giving.

Everything had broken. It was a hairline fracture in a pane of glass, which had cracked and split beneath the weight of the pills — only to eventually shatter completely, leaving nothing but shards to slice open one's skin.

And oh, but the world had taken those shards and split themselves open! Oh, but the world had seen the damage and leapt upon it with greed in their hearts! And Slater had been right there with them, so desperate to escape from his own plight and stress, he had not seen that it wasn't just his own flesh being rendered open. It was the flesh of everyone in Carnelian City.

It was the flesh of everyone who lived on their sordid path. And there was no way to fix it.

These were wounds that couldn't simply be stitched back together. There was no cure for the infection that had sunk deep into the Earth.

All around him, as he walked down the filthy cobbled streets, Slater was reminded of what had happened. How the introduction of the pills had changed things on a scale so great that there was no doubt no one had ever been able to predict it. It was in the countless empty houses. It was in the silence of the streets. It was in the aching, all pervasive loneliness.

Slater turned onto a street, stepping into what used to be the market district. Very few of the shops were still open. A young woman, not even thirty, sat on the cracked pavement in dirty clothes. The tips of her fingers were black as oil, like she'd stained them in ink.

Just the sight of it was enough to make Slater freeze.

A mistake, he quickly realized. The woman caught sight of his stillness and hurried to get up, though her stiff joints and weak limbs made that difficult. She was clutching a small bowl in one hand, empty with only a few coins, and crossed the street without looking.

A dented hovercar nearly ran her down, blaring its horn. The woman acted as though she had not even seen it.

"Sir," she said, her voice a rasp. "Have you anything to spare?"

Slater frowned. "I… know you from somewhere. What's your name?"

"Do you have anything to spare?" She repeated it with more urgency this time.

Slater reached into his wallet and pulled out a bill. The woman's eyes snapped to it, as though it was magnetized.

Once more, Slater demanded, "What's your name?"

"Maeve," she told him, with the air of someone who was no longer used to that name. "Maeve Marlowe."

"Maeve Marlowe," he echoed.

Slater's memory was getting spotty these days. He stood there a long moment, holding the bill tight in one hand, and thinking. Then it hit him. He made a soft "oh," one that was more air than sound.

Then he told her, "You used to own a grocery store."

Maeve nodded, just once. "I did. Is that for me, then?"

"It's for you," he told her, putting it into her bowl. "Do you know what happened to the baker who set up next to you?"

"Dead," she said, without missing a beat. There was no sorrow in Maeve's voice, not for him. Too much time had passed. Too much had changed. The generosity of Carnelian City had been ground out like a bug beneath a boot heel. "Nearly twenty years now."

"Oh," said Slater again, but with much less breath.

Maeve, having gotten her change, scuttled across the street without looking once more. She settled back down in her little corner of the world, eagerly running the bill between her black fingers.

The fact that the baker was dead, and Maeve was homeless, that should have churned Slater's stomach. But… it didn't. It was the sight of her fingers that made Slater feel ill.

He turned away from her, continuing down the road. One street. Two streets. His ill feeling would not abate. He thought about it.

That was a side effect of the pills, he knew.

Slater knew this because he had taken it. Had taken the pill amongst the few others who could afford it. And now, it was clear that the effects were starting to hit him.

Long ago, Slater had been a handsome hand. Even in his old age, his hair had been gray but thick. His fingers had ached but been straight. His skin had been pale but healthy. And now, the tips of his fingers were tinged with gray. It was the worst around his cuticles, where the pigmentation was so dark it was nearly black. But the rest of his fingers, up to that first joint near the nail, were ashen.

That color would darken. It would continue to grow filthier, blacker, until they resembled Maeve's fingers. And then the darkness would creep up to his knuckles, over his palms, staining his wrists and arms. Eventually, he would be as black as the world itself. As black as the corruption that had taken over the world itself. It would change him, and he would then no longer be the Slater that he had been before he took the pill. In fact, he hadn't been the same

Slater the minute he realized what taking the pill had done to him. People had a right to be angry with him for what he had done.

For the reason he had done it.

All that Slater had wanted — all he had changed for — was just to survive. He was infected, diseased, and dying. He didn't want to die because he was afraid of death, and yet he had done just that. He had done just that; he had bought, and then taken the pill, and eventually after fifty long years, he realized the utter horror that it had brought him, and that it had brought to his family.

Clayton died first. It was sudden. They mourned. Arlyne, the oldest grandchild, was picked up by Cryo Corps and swept away for ten years and then returned in a coffin to be buried, with nothing to his name, for Cryo Corps had claimed every invention as their own.

The youngest grandchild, Maia, lived to have a family of her own. But then an infectious sickness wiped them all out, one after the next.

And still, Slater lived.

Still, he lived, damn it all, and he would keep on living.

And if it wasn't bad enough to watch his family die, Slater knew with certainty that he would be here even when the entirety of their existence would die out. Living alone, with only a couple of other people who had taken the pill for the same reason as him. To live, to never die. And because of that, because of that greed and because of that utter terror of death, they were also turning.

Their kind was amazing. There were no skin colors, no discrimination, no difference between one man and the other. The only thing there was, was prosperity. Prosperity and contentment. Carnelian City had been the home of the future. Revolutionary. A true step toward a greater life!

But even beyond Carnelian City, the glow of the people could be seen. The Winding Roads connected worlds of all sorts, people from places so far away, it was barely even worth learning the names of the cities. Innovation was the priority of their kind; that's why the Cryo Corps was such a glinting gem in their society.

People were trying to take their light and bottle it. They were trying to find ways to further spread peace throughout the globe, to create new things constantly.

But the pills had changed it all.

The ability for someone to do whatever they wanted, but a simple pill had changed them all, and he for sure thought, in the end, that it was not worth it.

Slater turned onto another street and paused, struck for a moment by the sheer vast emptiness of Carnelian City. There were colorful confetti still caked into the brick work of some of these buildings, for there simply were not enough people left around to clean everything. And those who did remain didn't care the way that they used to.

At some point during the descent, there had been a riot. Several windows were broken; glass littered the sidewalk. The plants, no longer tended to, were riddled with weeds, and some of them had simply given up and died completely, sitting brown and gnarled in their white stone pots. It was just one more reminder of everything the pills had stripped out of the world.

Not only was humanity affected, but the world itself. And the stones! Once so white and dazzling that they glittered in the sun! Now, they were washed out. The pills had done something to the very atmosphere. Slater was no scientist. He couldn't say what the change was, not in so many words, anyway. But he knew it had happened. A faint grayness that clung to the air, blocking out what had once been pure, raw beauty.

Death clung to these stones, and it would not be forgotten.

Once more, Slater was forced to grapple with the fact that this was his fault. That he had a hand in this destruction by agreeing to take the pill. He had wanted a chance to change his life, but the change brought about had not been kind.

It was not worth taking the pill and having a chance to have it all. It was not worth taking the pill and having a chance to be on top of it all. It was not worth it to survive when everything else in the world hadn't.

Hindsight truly was 20/20.

Slater turned another corner, coming upon what had once been the park. The flowers had long since been overtaken by weeds and thorns. At the center of the park, stood a fountain. Years ago, it had been filled with water that crashed down in different colors; a stunning innovation that had drawn many lovers out to see it in the late hours of the night.

Slater went there now, even knowing that it had dried up. The power to it had been cut. Colorful stains riddled the basin of the fountain, a mark of what it used to be. With a heavy sigh, Slater sat down on the edge of the basin, letting his aching joints rest. He looked around, taking in the parts of the park that had been allowed to decay, and the parts that had been turned into a camp of sorts for the ill and the homeless.

Authorities didn't bother trying to police people anymore. Some of them lived here too, after all.

The pills had destroyed everyone. It had started slowly, a couple hundred losing their pale luster and beauty, their glow and their prosperity turning darker. They should have known it would happen. The team of scientists who had worked on the pills, they came out of those labs, black as sin! People had thought it was a result of failed experiments, not of the finished product! No one had realized that the pills would alter them on a fundamental level, leaving them stripped of their glow. And they hadn't realized that without their glow, they would struggle to maintain their health and humanity.

The pale luster faded, slowly at first, and then in great waves. Darker and darker and darker until it became difficult to even recognize them as beings and more as an existing personification of darkness, wrongness, greed, and nothingness. That was how dark they became. That was how dark the world was becoming. And as they grew darker, they lost greater and greater pieces of themselves. The symptoms differed sometimes, and so did the speed at which the change occurred. That's why Slater was only just starting to suffer from these ill effects himself.

But the people didn't care. They had ways and means of achieving whatever they wanted to achieve;

they had ways and means of achieving their dreams. That was all that they wanted.

So, what if they became walking shadows? Things of nightmares? Creatures that wore the suit of human flesh? So, what if time stood before them, immoral, and judging the vanity of these creatures?

They didn't care. They had no use for the world anymore.

The pills were all that they wanted, and the pills were all that they needed.

It didn't matter that the world was wasting away around them. It didn't matter that they, themselves, were wasting into husks. Dust in the form of a body. Hate in the form of a human body. It didn't matter.

No one cared anymore.

Even Slater had stopped caring.

It got to the point that every single day, darkness seemed to overtake the world. It wasn't even a metaphor. The more the humans lost their glow, the less the world itself seemed to be a bright and welcoming place. Like the stones that Slater now stood before, the world began to drift. The water no longer reflected the sun and sat still even on a windy day, and it tasted… foul. Even the clean water, it was just so sour, as if everything that had ever made it good was gone!

Elsewhere, the changes spread faster. People watched as trade routes fell apart. They watched as fights broke out. Forests withered. Animals suffered. It was the humans who had created the pills; it was the humans who had taken the pills, but it was not just the humans who suffered.

Slater shook his head and started walking once more. He tried not to think about it, but his mind had already strayed to these dark and heavy thoughts, and it seemed like it would be impossible to pull them free.

Once beautiful and amazing, the world was changing. Becoming a darker, worse place. Changing to something that was out of a sick nightmare rather than the dream their world used to be. It had crumbled around them like dust, and no one even tried to stop it.

And Slater had seen it with his very eyes. He had seen it, with his very own eyes, that the world, the people in this world, the best of all the people, were changing into something that was akin to a nightmare personified. Their darkness extended over, like a disease, corrupting the whole world around them, and Slater had seen what that corruption was leading to.

Their current state of being was a twisted version of reality. It was something that was a visible change.

Slater had known that it was happening. He had seen everything, and then some more.

And he had done nothing.

Worse than that, he had taken part in it.

Day by day, there were less people.

Week by week, more cities fell. People convened here, in Carnelian City; the last of them all, some homeless, some squatting, some like himself, clinging to riches that no longer had value. Many of them dead. Friends and family. The baker who lived down the street. Soon, Maeve. Soon, the people who lived in these empty tents, ghosts among a world filled with other ghosts.

And now, here he was, with a mere two hundred people, watching as the world itself was torn asunder. There was nothing left, for everything was turning dark. Everything was being lost to the blanket, the ocean of darkness that the pills had wrought down upon the world.

It had left the soil bitter. It had left the winds too harsh, the rains either too strong or too far between. Shadows had changed everything. They had burned the health and the compassion from the humans. The blanket of darkness was too much. The world couldn't survive it.

My god... Slater thought, tears falling down his eyes as despair took him.

And then as it took over him. He couldn't believe what was happening in front of him. Couldn't believe what had happened to the world in front of him. But then, it had been happening for fifty years now.

Why was Slater only just now seeing it?

Was that part of his curse? Was that part of what the pills had done to him, putting him in a world of blindness and distress? Pinning him here in a box with a cloak, and only letting him be aware of the damage now that it was too late to do anything about it?

Sickness swept through him. Bile bit at the back of Slater's teeth, and he had to stop and take a deep breath, trying to fight the queasiness down. He could barely breathe through it — this awful sickness. Blackness swam in the corner of his vision. Slater shook his head, hard, and breathed sharply through his nose until the panic and sickness faded away.

Once the world of pure and utter happiness and content, now was a world of utter destruction, death, and mayhem. It was the world where one couldn't exist without being corrupted. Like he was being corrupted. Like he was also changing.

This sickness was abated for the moment, but it would take him soon enough. And wouldn't that be worse than death? Slater feared that it might have been. There was no one around to ask, though.

Once more, his gaze went to his hands. He held them up, looking them over. Turned them first this way and then that way, curling each finger one at a time, one at a time, and counting them as he did. One. Two. Three. He still wore the wedding band he'd gotten from his wife. Four. Five. Six. That finger had a scar on it. What was it from?

Slater frowned. His memory was like a sieve these days. He had to fight to try and get the thought back, but he soon forgot what he was trying to fight.

For a long time, Slater stared at his finger. Then he forgot what he was staring at and started to count again. One. Two. Three. The ring from his dead wife. Four. Five. Six. Seven. Eight. Nine. Ten.

Oh.

Oh!

Had his fingers been this dark even just a few moments ago? Slater was certain that the answer was no. The tips were black as ink. The fingers a ruddy gray halfway up. His thumbs, shorter than the rest, were almost completely gray.

The change would happen fast, now that he'd started. It would take him quickly. Maybe that was for the best. At least, that meant his awareness would be stripped away soon enough.

It seemed that finally, he would have to pay the price, watching the ever-rising blanket of darkness overtaking the devastated world, slowly, every second by second, overtaking the world in its long-reaching grasp. He didn't want that to happen. But he couldn't avoid it. He had been one of the people who had helped it nurture and grow, after all.

The pill had been swallowed. No one forced Slater to take it. It had been placed on his tongue and slid down his gullet at his own will.

And now, he paid the price, being absorbed by the ever-lasting darkness. Once again, he didn't want to, but he had no choice.

It was going to be a slow, agonizingly slow, process, but he would be there to feel every single second of it, until he was as dark as this corrupted world had become. And all he could do was curse them. Curse the creators of the pills.

And curse all those, like himself, who took it.

Chapter Two

THIS WORLD WAS A WONDERFUL PLACE. It was a simple fact, one that everyone knew, and one that most people agreed with. Anyone could come out and say that. Admit that it was a wonderful place. That the world was filled with kindness and areas where it was easy to breathe and simply live as yourself. Poverty was at an all-time low. Suicide rates had dropped down to almost nothing. Peace had settled over the land like a blanket, and the world was taking comfort in that.

But like every existence, there was strife. There was calamity, and there was destruction. Every coin had two sides, after all.

Some people had it good, living in societies that were cooperative. Carnelian City was one of the most well-known places, a city that thrived by helping others. No one would go hungry there, no one would be unhappy there, and no one would be sad there. But some of the world didn't have such a pleasure.

Aether Heights was a city on the far side of the Southern Hemisphere, and while it was fully developed, it was a tragedy. Crime was higher there than anywhere else in the world. People argued and fought — not because they needed to, but because they wanted resources; they wanted to be the first to achieve new things!

And as they fought, their city suffered. That became an issue.

That was a part of the world that simply didn't have the happiness and satisfaction that Carnelian City had. And that part vastly overtook the happiness of the much more developed parts of the world.

So, the various influential people in the world came up with an idea. They knew that the world could not continue like this. Or rather, they decided that they wouldn't let it. They would need to make a change, so that there were more places like Carnelian City. So that the entire world could be like Carnelian City — a utopian dream, a loving community.

They decided that they had to make something that could help them counter their problems, help them counter the potential destruction they were facing. It was not because of jealousy, but because they had to save their people, save their homes and their families. It was what they wished to do, and they were going to succeed.

And while the politicians of the world weren't able to do anything at the moment, they knew that if they put some effort into it, they would be able to change that. They started to gather together funds, mapping out their thoughts.

Hence, that was why the scientists had decided to meet up and start working on a project that would help them solve this strife. In the form of pills. Actual pills that would help them out in gaining whatever they wanted, and give them the power to do whatever they needed to do. It had seemed far-fetched to some, and the world had balked at the idea. After all, such a thing couldn't truly come into being, right?

Their plan was much more difficult than what they were used to, but with their technology and their brains, the scientists were confident that they could do it. It didn't matter that everyone else had decided it was impossible. This collection of the most brilliant were used to doing the impossible. They had spent years studying how to make advancements in their world, and now, this was going to be their chance to do exactly that!

The governing forces had given them ample money as well, allotting monthly funds to fuel the project. It was thought that this pill might be able to bring about world peace — something that even their glittering, glowing world had yet to achieve.

And because of that, it was their single largest priority.

The scientists were fully focused on their project. Many of them locked themselves away in the lab that they'd been given. If they had families, they stopped seeing them. Some of them stopped going home altogether. Slowly, these people began to change.

If one were to look at the scientists, the first thing they would notice was, unlike the rest of the world who all had pure white glowing skin and features, they had gray, almost black, skin. Their pale robes were heavily contrasting with their skin, and they seemed as if they were causing the entire world around them to have a destructive aura by just existing.

It wasn't just their skin. Their eyes grew darker and darker, until there was no white left in them. Their hair thinned. Some of them had twists forming in their fingers, as if the gravity of the world was affecting the state of their muscles and joints, pushing them into a different form. But the scientists didn't care. They kept up with their research.

It was no longer a project. It had become more than just a fascination. It had become an obsession. They were going to create this pill and change the state of the world, no matter what happened.

One such woman was Veronica Sins, the head scientist in the investigation for the correct formula of the pill in question. She was almost always in a state of agitation these days — for three years, she had been leading this project, searching for a cure to end strife completely, searching for the formula that would lead her team to success and herself into a position of eternal fame.

And yet, so far, there had been nothing.

Veronica's office was a rather bland space. It had a large, hardwood desk which held a state-of-the-art computer, a single plastic succulent, and one stack of papers. The papers were a new addition, brought in twenty minutes ago by one of Veronica's prized aids, Caroline Pierce. They had already been picked up and read twice, only to be tossed back down onto the desk. With each read, the stack became more unkempt and unorganized.

Veronica paced from one side of the office to the other, back and forth. She did this so often, it was a true wonder that she hadn't yet worn an actual gorge into the floor! The sound of her white boots click-clacking against the white tiles filled the office. The cadence didn't match up with Veronica's heartbeat, which seemed loud enough to serve as a drum line.

Back and forth, back and forth. She raked a hand through her thinning red hair. At almost forty, Veronica was far from the beauty of her youth — and her recent physical changes hadn't helped. As her skin took on a darker, ink-like color, her hair had begun to fall out, and the joints in her fingers had started to ache.

She assumed that it was stress and arthritis catching up to her — one more reason that she needed to make certain this formula was completed quickly. If she could finish this pill, she could take it herself — erasing all the strife that had settled into her being.

Veronica shook her head, raking her hand through her hair a second time, and then scrubbing at her face with her palm. "Ridiculous! This is absolutely ridiculous! There's no reason that should have failed!"

She grabbed the papers up a second time, several of them slipping from the stack and fluttering down onto the floor. Veronica ignored them in favor of raking her gaze over the stack of papers again, pulling in one breath and then another. There was a budding headache at the back of her skull, the threat of a migraine that would soon be full blown.

Veronica gnashed her teeth together, biting the inside of her cheeks in the process. Although she could taste blood where her molars had split the spongy flesh, she felt no pain from the nip. She was so focused on reading over the papers a third time that nothing else seemed to exist.

"No, that is the wrong formula. It won't work!" This time, when Veronica threw the stack of papers, the better part of them didn't even make it onto the desk. They fluttered onto the floor instead, where they were quickly ground up under the heels of her white boots as she began her pacing and stamping once more. "Why? Why is this so difficult?"

It shouldn't have been! The brightest minds in the world were put on this project, with near unlimited funding! This was something that they should have been able to figure out! It should already have been made!

Veronica snarled, "This is getting ridiculous!"

Her reason for snapping? The experimentation reports that she was reading. Like many of the reports that showed up in her office, this one didn't bring good news. It brought yet another failure.

Each entry in this experimentation report shows the report of one single subject that was tested with a prototype of the pill. Every single entry is a new patient and a new prototype.

Because of lack of time, we have skipped the gender, the height, weight, and age of the patients and subjects. We have included all entries currently available, including those that have previously been sent in for your consideration.

Entry 1:

Catastrophic failure. The spinal column broke due to the strength of the pill. The subject was unable to survive the injury and had to be put down. It took several hours for the full break to occur, but the process itself was slow and drawn out. The cracks began at the center of the spine and pushed outward, vertically, without splitting all the way through, before growing horizontally. By the end of five hours, there was too much surface destruction for the bones to hold up; they split all the way through.

The result was a waste of resources and a waste of a subject. We must make progress at a faster pace. This is the first time that the spine has been damaged so severely, but we're also not seeing any of the results we want. Our benefactors will begin to grow unhappy if we aren't able to present them with some form of result shortly. We must drastically change the composition during the next test.

Recommendation: New formula. Failure to be expected at early stages. Must find new test subjects as well as new areas to properly integrate the pill into. Reminder, pill is meant to end strife, not cure a disease. This pill must have the power to change reality, therefore Nano-technological and Dark Matter Manipulative Technology must be used. While these are both experimental subjects, they cannot be excluded from our research in the proper formula for the pill. A balance between them and the natural state of a human body must be found.

Entry 2:

Catastrophic failure. Complete organ shut down. This formula did not damage the spine, which was originally thought to be a success. However, within the first twenty-four hours of administering the first dose of the pill, it became clear that the body was treating it as an invasive subject and reacting accordingly. Originally, this only impacted the kidneys — something that could have been countered both with treatment and with a slight alteration to the formula of the pill.

By the thirty-ninth hour, the shutdown of organs had begun to spread, affecting the kidneys, liver, lungs, and spleen. There was no sign that it would be contained to these organs and continued to spread over the progression of a total forty-eight hours. The subject was terminated at that point, as there would be no way to secure or continue studies with it.

Recommendation: New formula. Subject also showed signs of dementia as well as heavy mutation. Must find a new line-up for Nano-Particles. The pill's inner makeup is easily mixing in with human blood. However, one of the biggest problems is the blood is becoming corrosive with the amount of nano-particles that are being absorbed. This power must be contained somehow or else it will never work. Research into absorbing particles should be prioritized.

Entry 3:

Catastrophic Failure. Subject showed no signs of response to the pill. Completely ineffective. First subject to not react catastrophically with Nano-Particles. While this was a failure for our study into the pill, it did provide us with important information in regards to how Nano-Particles might be altered so that they can accurately function inside of a living subject. The pill itself had no effect on the subject, but there was also no negative result. Kept aside for further experimentation after permission from patient.

Side Note: Subject showed signs of recovery from Leukemia. Could this be used to further medical advancements in other parts of the field? The pill is not designed to cure health ailments but to erase strife, but I see no reason why sects of these discoveries should not be utilized elsewhere, to counter problems that, as of yet, have no cure. I will pass these notes along to a co-worker in a different field, so that they might get some further use.

Recommendation: New formula with old one set aside for medical study. This pill has shown success in a medical aspect but not in the aspect that will solve the problem at hand. Formula and inner makeup must be changed again. A recommendation to save this formula and submit it to the medical research team has already been noted and carried out. However, regardless of the accidental success, no progress has been made using this formula.

Scientists were constantly altering the formula and then trying again, working at fixing up a new section of the problem. They pulled every tip, trick, and alteration that they could come up with, and then they continued to test on vulnerable subjects, with or without their consent.

Every single test either failed or had no effect. All of their test subjects started dying, and things were... not going as plan, to tell the truth. It was hard to believe. They had the best equipment in the world, the best technological advancements that would help them create this pill. They had funds. They had time. They had everything... but the solution seemed to remain just out of reach.

Veronica couldn't stand it! Every single page in that stack was just further proof that she had failed — that her team had failed. For three years, they had been working on this project, and they had so little to show for it! Some might consider the discovery about how Nano-Technology could be used in the medical field to be a boon, but Veronica didn't see it that way. They weren't looking to aid in the research of others.

Their tests only had one goal — to erase strife. To design a pill that would change the world in ways the average human could barely perceive to be possible. Veronica had been tasked with making the dreams of the richest people in the world become reality, and it felt as though there were eyes on her constantly, waiting for some sort of a report. Even when she was at home, Veronica was haunted by this task.

Because the creation of the pill would be so earth-shattering, every news channel seemed to be running daily debates on the subject. They asked questions about the safety and ethics, trying to figure out if it was even possible for Dark Matter and time to be altered, and then trying to figure out if it was worth it.

As if they knew anything!

Veronica had spent her entire life studying Dark Matter. She had worked for Cryo Corps, and now, she was leading this project — and still, there was so much about the subject that Veronica didn't know, that she could never hope to fully understand.

The idea of talk show hosts acting as though they understood even an iota of this project was almost laughable.

They had gloves that could manipulate Dark Matter and particles in real time. It was something that had never been available before. In fact, the gloves had been created specifically for the purpose of these tests, for it had been determined that Dark Matter was going to be the key to creating the pills. Being able to manipulate it was critical to their experiments.

They had ways and means of properly creating Dark Matter itself, the only power known to have ways and means to alter reality inside of their labs. They had the brightest experts in the whole world to help them create this pill, but it wasn't going as well as they'd expect. They did everything in their power, everything to succeed.

But things were going really bad, both in the lab and outside the lab. With each month that passed by, tension began to pull tighter and tighter. Many of the people involved in the project had quit. They lost all contact with the outside world. This project was the only thing that remained.

That's how it was for Veronica, too. And yet, no matter what they did, they seemed no closer to coming up with the formula that they needed.

It had been over three years since they started their project. Three years of failure upon failure, and disappointment upon disappointment. The pill was no closer to being created now than it had been all those years ago.

And with each failed attempt, it was Veronica's name that got brought up. Veronica's name that was featured in disparaging headlines, brought up in debates on live television, becoming a commodity in the homes of people who had barely graduated high school. Fame was one thing that Veronica had always wanted. Craved it, even.

Veronica wanted her name to be one that would never be forgotten!

Just... not for this. Not for failure to create the pill. There was so much sitting on Veronica's shoulders right now, and with each passing day, that weight seemed to press down harder against her. The very first subject they tested the pill on, his spine had broken. Sometimes, it felt as though Veronica's spine will snap and splinter the same way, just giving out fully under the pressures of those around her.

The strife in the countries that didn't have the co-operation that the bigger, more advanced countries did was growing, and the world was threatened with wars and destruction. Each day, more corruption seemed to be outed. This politician was lying. That country was creating more bombs. Their way of being was threatened in a way that they didn't know if it would survive the oncoming future or not. It was going so bad that the scientists were afraid the war would end the world before they could come up with their finished product.

Veronica did her best to rally her team, giving them the motivation to move forward.

"We're the last chance our world has," said Veronica at one conference meeting. "If we can't make this pill, there's no telling how much longer society will last. We are, truly, the last barrier standing between perfection and destruction."

Veronica knew it was the truth, and so did the other scientists working on the project with her.

So, they galloped, they started to work harder, and harder, and harder, and they came up with something to help them out. It was the 180th patient that showed the signs of success. 180th.

Word of that would spread in no time! Even though Veronica tried to keep things under wraps, it was virtually impossible to do so. Everyone who worked in the labs had signed a confidentiality agreement of the highest sort the day they had been hired. And yet, somehow, the reporters always knew about the latest failure.

Was there a mole among her employees? Were one of their computers bugged? It was frustrating, even more so that Veronica didn't have an answer for the question.

Veronica raked a hand through her hair again, and then grabbed hold of a chunk of it, tugging at the thinning locks until she could feel the bright bursts of pain shooting across her scalp.

"Focus," she told herself. "That doesn't matter. The only thing of any importance is figuring out how to make progress."

Veronica forced herself back to her desk, only to realize quite suddenly and for the first time, that the papers were scattered on the floor instead. Veronica swore in every language she knew — twelve of them, to be exact — before lowering herself down onto her knees and beginning to search through the scattered sheets of paper for the one that she needed. It contained the information on their most recent attempts at designing a working formula for the pill.

Veronica let out a sigh when she found it, hauling herself up onto her feet. In an effort to prevent anymore temper tantrums or outbursts, she stepped around the side of her desk and sat down on the large, plush chair. Veronica shook out the paper and then settled in to read it again.

Entry 180:

Partial Success. The makeup of the pill and the proper instillation of Dark Matter has made a successful combination that alters reality around the patient. However, this was only a partial success because after a few minutes, the reality around the patient broke down and caused instant death. The breakdown of reality was only just visible, appearing as a distortion in the air, much like a heat haze. This distortion pressed inward and crushed the patient physically.

Recommendation: Serum needs to be reworked. We have figured out a proper base for the materials used in the pill. Proper particle manipulation has allowed the Dark Matter and Nano-Technology to properly interact with each other and manipulate reality as per the desire of the patient. However, because of the instantaneous manipulation of reality, it is not adhering. At times, the pill stops being effective, and at times, it kills the patient. It is advised to change the instantaneous process of the pill into a gradual one. This formula was a success, now time to augment it properly. It is also to be noted that the formula is getting too large and may cause overheating problems in the future. The use of a different base is advised.

Second Recommendation: Augment the base of the formula and simply restructure it.

It was the next part that really made her furious and extremely annoyed for no particular reason. The main problem in it all? The serum simply was breaking down reality instead of manipulating it, no matter what type of a formula they used or what they did.

Veronica was in charge of the project. Any changes to the formula had to be run past her. And the most recent entry… it made her teeth ache with fury, a sort of biting and irrational anger that she'd been suffering from a lot recently. It was the stress getting to her, Veronica was sure of it.

Trying to resist the urge to simply shred the paper into a thousand pieces, Veronica took a deep breath and turned her gaze to the ceiling. She took another deep breath and counted backwards from ten.

By the time she hit the end of the count down, she felt no less settled. Oh, well. She supposed that it was worth the try. She took another deep breath, and then looked down at the paper once more.

Entry 181:

Subject didn't show aptitude to the serum, and instead, instantly got a stroke and passed away due to a massive hemorrhage. It is impossible to calculate which patient will be affected by the rapid reality-manipulating powers of the pill, or not be affected at all by the pill. This is causing major dissonance amongst the project backers and funders. A total of two hundred patients has already died due to this particular experiment. It will be wise to terminate the project, but surprised backing from various governments have revived it again. New formulas are already in the works.

This was the shortest entry in the set. The most recent one. Veronica stared at it, hating the suggestion to terminate the project, hating the fact that they couldn't. There were no good options. Even now, a part of Veronica knew that this project would not end smoothly. There were so many deaths already attributed to it. So much blood had been spilled in their labs, and so much more would no doubt splatter onto the floor before time was up.

And yet, Veronica could not doubt it. She couldn't say a single disparaging word against the project. Their funding was still coming in by the handfuls, and the entire world was locked onto Veronica. If she showed doubt... well, it just wasn't a possibility.

So, Veronica did the only thing that she could.

The lead scientist of the project gave into the anger that was brewing inside of her like a storm, and she finally let herself rip the paper into tiny, little pieces. And then she ripped up all the other papers, picking them up off the floor, one by one, and shredding them between her night black fingers. A small part of Veronica's brain was surprised that she didn't leave a stain on everything she touched, but the darkness never bled out of her skin.

By the time each page had been shredded, it looked a little bit like snow on the ground. Snow. Winter. What month was it? What season? For a split second, Veronica wasn't sure. They had been working on this project for three years, but what day of the week was it?

She turned toward her desk, where a calendar used to be, but found nothing. Uneasiness began to brew in the back of Veronica's chest. Something important felt out of place — but the feeling was gone before she could fully grasp onto it, slipping through her fingers like water through a sieve.

It didn't matter, in the end. Veronica couldn't linger and try to figure out what was wrong. She had important work to do.

Time passed. Another year, to be exact. The project to discover a way to end strife continued, and Veronica continued to lead it. They went from Entry 181 all the way to Entry 392. Or, as it was more commonly known, to the 392nd subject.

Entry 392:
The pill is properly working, gradually manipulating reality under the control of a singular base desire of the mind. Formula is such that the reality bubble surrounding a single person does not

interfere with another subject who has taken the pill. Every single type of experiment has one single disadvantage: the patient, in the end, is corrupted. Darkening of the skin and then death is usual, but this particular product is a success. Research on how to perfect it has been postponed for quick release of the product in the market.

This is strongly advised against; I'm certain that advice will go unheeded, but it's now documented all the same. There is still much that isn't known about Dark Matter. We will continue to research its effects on the human body as we refine and fast track the pill for its release.

It was the 392nd patient that had shown success; however, that wasn't the end of it. Oh, no, it wasn't the end of it. They had to do simulation runs. Still, they were closer now than they had been in almost four years. Veronica could taste the success. Her previous concerns regarding morality were gone. She was wholly focused on the project at hand.

Some would say that Veronica had even become obsessed with it.

After all, her own life was filled with strife! Shouldn't she be allowed to want a cure for that? Once this pill was completed, Veronica had decided that she would be one of the first people to take it.

So, she cleared the simulations without even pausing to think about the ramifications. The drawbacks. The fact that these were real living humans she was about to subject to Dark Matter and possibly unethical experiments; there was no one watching them, no one checking in to make sure they were following protocol.

Every day, the news reported on the project, but the articles had all taken a positive spin over the last three months. The world could tell that Veronica and her crew of scientists were close to figuring things out.

So, the simulations were approved.

The simulations all showed manners of success, but in the 393rd patient till the 399th patient, they realized that the pills weren't working for longer than ten minutes. It was the same problem that was going on before, the pills would stop having an effect after just ten minutes.

Something was wrong with it. Was it the pill? The formula? There was a possibility that the human body simply wasn't capable of withstanding the effects of the pill for any longer without being reduced to a crumpling, failed pile of flesh and blood. That was a possibility Veronica quickly brushed aside.

Veronica flung the most recent report across her office and stormed out the room. The hall of the labs was white and large; the sound of her boots echoed. Due to the nature of the experiments, each individual room had been sound-proofed so that the simulation in one room couldn't disturb the research taking place in another.

The light was so glaringly bright that it made her luminescent robe shuffle and shimmer about, draped over her, loose and sunken in form. Veronica didn't remember the last time that she had stepped outside of the labs. She no longer went home at night, choosing instead to sleep on a cot that had been brought into her office, with a thin cotton blanket and an even more uncomfortable pillow.

Veronica stormed down the hallway to the office that belonged to her most trusted sect of the team; Allie Redoubt, Sigs Kuhns, and Josiah Stone were just as invested in the project as Veronica was. She flung open the door to their office with enough force that it bounced loudly off the wall. The three scientists inside, startled.

"We have to do something about this problem. *Something!*" Veronica snarled. "So, please, get to work, or we'll be showing the backers our empty hands!"

"Ma'am, I think we may have some success," Allie said suddenly, looking up. "It's not much to look at, but it is definitely some success in the right direction!"

"Anything at this point, I'll take," Veronica replied, asking for her file. "Show me."

"Yes, ma'am." The other scientist, Sigs, nodded, passing the file. "I've been experimenting on patient number 400, and I've had some serious success. As you can see… I manipulated the base structure a bit."

"You used the Nano-Particles as a liquid instead of a solid?" Veronica asked, looking back at the scientist. "Is this… a real test?"

"Yes." Sigs nodded. "It is. You can look at the videos yourself. No matter how much I try to prove it wrong, I feel that this is it. This is the proper formula to use. The problem of eventual Dementia still exists, but this is what we wanted to create."

"This is ground-breaking," said Veronica. "Why wasn't I informed of this sooner?"

"The results are just from this morning."

"I don't care when they're from," yelled Veronica. "They should have been brought to me immediately!"

The people in the room were all the same. Their constant exposure to Dark Matter had stripped the glow from their skin. It made their bodies take on the darkness of the material that they worked with. With the four of them gathered in this room, it seemed a bit like their flesh was absorbing the light.

Despite the fact that this room was no dimmer than the rest of the hallway had been, the shadows here seemed thicker. The very presence of these people seemed to be altering the world around them — but it went unnoticed. That was the flaw in the minds of scholars, you know. They could never see when they crossed a line. Their entire life had been narrowed into a pin-prick moment, where nothing mattered outside of the completion of this task.

"It won't happen again," said Sigs.

Allie added, "We've been watching the patient around the clock and so far, he's shown no signs of ill effects. This might really be the thing that we've been looking for. We could be on the precipice of really discovering something."

"I won't stay on the precipice for long," warned Veronica. "I want to know one way or another whether or not this formula will be a success. A liquid! I've never even thought about that!"

"It's not wholly on me," said Sigs. "Josiah was reading an article from someone at Cryo Corps—"

Veronica interrupted, "I want that article on my desk within the hour."

Josiah said, "It's not about Dark Matter. Some kid from Carnelian City, he's working on designing a new fuel for the power plants. And he mentioned changing the base matter, and that's when I started thinking about how, for all the changes we've done, we've only ever tried to use solid Dark Matter. Changing it to liquid…"

"It worked," said Allie, firmly.

Sigs was quick to say, "We don't know if it worked just yet. I'm not going to have any of us jumping in with both feet, and then having to deal with the fall out. All we know is that it made a difference."

Allie argued, "This patient is still alive, and for all that we can tell, the pill has done what it's supposed to do."

Sigs insisted, "And we won't know if it will last until we finish running our tests."

"You're both right," said Veronica with a wave of her hand. She jabbed a finger first at Josiah, reiterating, "I don't care what the original article was about. I want it on my desk within the hour, and then I want a written report of how you came to the conclusion to alter the base state into a liquid form."

Josiah nodded, "Yes, ma'am. I'll make sure to get them both to you immediately."

He turned in his chair, already grabbing his pen and paper to start documenting the line of thoughts and queries that led him to try out this new test run.

Veronica spun around, turning back to face the other two. She jabbed a finger at Sigs. "And you, details. I want details. Written, oral, both. Allie, with me."

She spun around and left the office without waiting for a response, knowing that Allie would follow. They stepped back into the hallway, and she led her to the viewing window of the 400th patient.

Through the window, Veronica was able to see inside the room. Two entire walls were made from computers, and the third wall was made from devices meant to help stabilize the universe should the process fail and the pill self-destruct, as it had done on many of their previous attempts.

The bed in the room was a simple, bare gurney. A tall, skinny man lied on the gurney, wearing nothing but the simple slip of a hospital gown. His skin was already starting to turn gray, and the whites of his eyes had become so black that it made his blue pupils stand out stark in contrast.

He sat on the bed with his arms folded on his lap, seemingly staring at nothing. A series of wires was connected to his left arm, and more to both his neck and his chest; they had to constantly measure everything. The wall filled with computers displayed screens that were constantly flickering about, monitors that were changing, and counts that didn't stay the same for more than a half second at a time.

"Incredible," said Veronica, in awe of the sight before her. "I was starting to think—"

"You can say it," said Allie. She was a tall and petite woman. The dark hues that her skin had taken on made her ashy blonde hair seem as though it had been bleached of every last once visible copper tone. "We were all thinking it. Nearly four hundred patients, and none of them had adhered. Not until this one. We were all starting to wonder if there was any point."

"And now, here it is," chimed Veronica. "Our divine intervention, of a sort." She chuckled. "To think, we could have done this ages ago if we had only thought a little further outside the box."

Allie asked her, "Do you know what tests you want run first?"

"I'll have an answer for you once I finish reading my reports," said Veronica. "In the meantime, keep monitoring him. I want him under a constant watch, is that understood?"

Allie nodded, and the two went their separate ways. As requested, both reports were on her desk within an hour, and as she read them, Veronica became more certain that they had finally found the missing link.

All they had to do now was run a clinical study.

And that's just what the group did. They ran all sorts of tests on the 400th patient and did whatever they could do to make sure nothing would go horribly wrong if introduced to the market. And it didn't.

It didn't!

They had done it. They had finally, after months upon months of research, finally succeeded in creating a pill that was actually working, and all of them couldn't be happier about it. Happier and happier until their very hearts pained from the sheer happiness that they were feeling. But that wasn't the end of it. That wasn't the end of it at all.

Four hundred people had died before they were able to reach the proper success. Four hundred people had lost their lives for this experimental dream to come true. No one would ever say that out in the open, but the scientists had managed to make a pill that could properly change reality, that could properly change the world in such a way that it was still difficult to believe.

Veronica was the one who gave the live speech on TV about the results, and from there, it was on the front cover of every newspaper and magazine. It was the only thing covered on radio shows and televised talk shows. There was no one in the world who didn't know the name of Veronica Sins and her team!

Finally, Veronica went home.

It had been too long since she stepped into her house. The air was riddled with the reek stench of dust and mustiness. She opened a window, but the sunshine didn't seem capable of coming in through the glass. It hit Veronica's skin and seemed to shy back outside, like a skittish animal refusing entry.

That didn't matter.

Veronica's brain was stuck on the fact that after so many years and so much sacrifice, they had finally succeeded. She walked almost numb through her home, stepping into the shower and feeling the heat of it roll over her bare skin.

Veronica looked at her palms and then at her body, where the glimmering white glow had been leeched away.

"There *is* beauty in this," she decided, but the words felt hollow. "And even if there's no beauty in it, there's power in it."

There. That second part tasted better on her tongue.

"There is power and fame," said Veronica to the empty bathroom. She scrubbed her dark skin and washed her thinning hair, and when she got out, instead of drying herself, she stood in front of the mirror and said it again. "Money and fame. By God, you lunatic, you've finally managed to do it. All this time, and you've finally managed to get it done. Fucking incredible."

Her reflection didn't answer. It just stared back at Veronica, letting her take in the true depth of her transformation for the very first time. The whites of her eyes were black as night, and her skin was even blacker. It wasn't like ink anymore. The color had grown more solid, had become deeper. It seemed to devour any light that touched it rather than reflect it.

Her pigment was more than a shadow now, and more than the night of the sky. Her hair was thinning, and sometimes, her hands shook. It was hard to remember things — she hadn't taken the pill yet, but the exposure to Dark Matter had not been kind to her. Especially in those early days when they were still trying to figure out what was going wrong and how it should be handled.

Sometimes, it felt like her brain was leaking memories. Veronica believed it was just strife, and she was certain the pill would fix it.

Bracing one hand against the marble countertop, not noticing that it had turned dark beneath her fingers, Veronica leaned closer to the mirror. She used her other hand to reach up and pull her lower lids down away from her eyeballs. Two years ago, there would have been blood vessels visible. Now though, the black covered even that.

"It's worth it," Veronica decided, leaning back.

She washed her hands and then went into the living room, where she turned on her television and was met with her own face staring back at her, reciting information about the pill, what it did, how it worked.

She didn't mention any risks.

She didn't plan on ever mentioning them.

And a month after their success, it hit the markets.

Chapter Three

WHEN SOMETHING DID HIT THE markets, a lot of things were usually involved in it. Most of all, was the market research a company would do, and then all other manners of promotional discounts, advertisement, and a build-up of a positive reputation.

First, they would get an announcement. People talking about the pending release on the news, fold outs and advertisements in magazines. It wouldn't be uncommon to hear jingles for it on the radio, or have paid sponsors talking about how it changed their life and would change your life, too. There was a method to the madness — a method to convincing people to purchase their new, and possibly ill-tested and poorly-executed, product. It was a method that had been around since people first started selling wares.

Even years and years ago, during the Gold Rush that was nearly forgotten, people had pitches for their clients. Snake oil salesmen had routines that they went through, and specific points they covered to convince people to buy their fake medicine. And it worked!

If sellers were convincing enough, then they could make the people around them purchase damn near anything. They would go against their common sense to buy something with bright enough and consistent enough advertisements, even if they knew it was a risk that might come back to bite them in the ass.

So, it was no wonder that fancy advertisements filled with bright colors had become the norm in regards to releasing new products. It had become the expectation.

The pills, however, had no such thing. They had just one advertisement of them running in the markets, and everything, and everyone, went wild.

The advertisement itself was simple. It was a straight-forward commercial that covered the fact that the pills were officially being launched, as well as the date of launch and where they were sold. There were no frills or animatics to go with it; it was just a woman in a pretty blue dress sitting on a stool, with a white background, holding a pitch-black pill.

She told them what the pill did, but only in brief. The mystery was intriguing. There was a disclosure at the bottom of the screen, but the writing was too small, the paragraph too large, and the movement of it too fast for anyone to actually read it. Whatever warnings might have been given were, effectively, kept completely secret.

That should have been a warning to people. They should have realized that the lack of full disclosure meant there would be a catch — but they didn't. When faced with the possibility of having their dreams come true, they didn't even stop to question what might happen to them if they took it. They didn't stop to wonder why there was so little fluff or hoopla put into releasing it.

The advertisement said that the pills were perfection in a capsule, and the entire world believed it.

People flocked to the nearest government building, where the pills were going to be sold, to get them because who didn't want to complete their desire and dreams? Who didn't want to have their life's goals completed, with virtually no effort put in on their end? With no drawbacks? With nothing at risk except for the hefty price of the pills themselves? It seemed like a miracle come true, and no one was willing to look at something like that, scoff, and deny it. No one would look at such a gift and turn it away.

Suddenly, things that would never have been possible were right there at the tips of the common man's fingers! It was within their reach! Their dreams, their goals, anything and everything that they could ever want, they could have!

And the biggest vantage point of them all? It worked. It actually worked. There were no side effects, there were no adverse effects, and there were no idiotic attempts of trying to discredit it.

That disclaimer at the bottom of the commercial was effectively forgotten.

If this was a medication, people would have done their research. They would have made sure that disclaimer was read, translated into the common tongue, and became popular knowledge. But the pills were different.

These weren't just a cure for a sickness. They were a cure for strife. They promised peace and comfort in a way that nothing else presently existing could manage. They were hope unbridled.

Why would anyone turn that away?

What one wanted, was being completed. What one wanted, was being granted.

How could people want to dissect that, to prove it false? It spread like wildfire. And the more people bought the pills and got their success, the more others wanted to try it for themselves. They could see the difference it was making in the world, even just by the end of the first week. People were more successful than ever. They were smarter, kinder, happier. They were achieving things that would have otherwise taken years to achieve — maybe even their whole lives!

It was as though the world was a puzzle, and the pills were the last piece needed to make the picture complete.

But there were some who didn't approve. These were very small sects, mind you, and many of them had a heavy religious background. Many groups said it was wrong to do so, that the pills were actually an attempt at playing God. Various religious groups called for boycotts and called for not using the pills.

It was… oddly ineffective.

In the past, the groups might have been able to get media coverage — but now, the common people only heard about them from a friend of a friend, or if they knew someone who was actively involved. These groups were such a minority that the television stations, even the local ones, had no interest in covering them. There was nothing about them on the radio or the news.

For every speech disavowing the pills that the groups managed to get heard by people, seventeen more came out touting how amazing the pills were, how helpful, how life changing, how perfect. It was that perfection that the rest of the world clung to. They saw the silver lining and nothing else, turning a blind eye to those who wanted to prevent the pill from being passed around at a higher rate.

The words of those who opposed the pills fell on deaf ears. Often, it resulted in the members of those organizations being mocked and laughed at, sometimes, in their buildings being defaced. They tried to use that as a point to argue their opinion even more — did those who reacted in this manner truly deserve to play God?

But no one would listen. No one wanted to hear about how these pills might actually not have been fit for public consumption. They certainly didn't want to discuss the restrictions being placed on who could have access to the pills. If anything, they wanted the pills to be even more readily available!

Faced with the option of being left behind, the groups who had been opposing the pills gave up quicker than they ever had given up before.

And the people benefited. It was ridiculous, something out of a dream, something that had never been seen before. People, all manner of people, let it be child or senior citizen, let it be male or female, let it be rich or poor, everyone was able to buy these pills, and everyone was able to complete their dreams. And it got to such a point, such a big point, that it became difficult for someone to live without them.

They couldn't see how it would be possible!

In fact, they could no longer understand how it had been possible before! These pills caused such a drastic change in the lives of those who took them that they could no longer remember what it had been like to put hard work into something, to see achievement and success come from years and years of dedication. They could no longer remember what it felt like to fail.

And really, why was that something they would hold onto?

No one wanted to remember the shame of being unable to reach their dreams. No one wanted to recall what it had been like to struggle their entire lives, only to effectively get nowhere. Their entire focus was on these pills, and on how these pills were truly helpful to them; how with these pills, they could accomplish anything that they wanted. Hell, they could accomplish *everything* that they wanted!

And so, people ignored the parts that did go wrong.

For as with everything that seemed to be perfection… it really *was* too good to be true. Oddly enough, things didn't fall apart because a strange side effect began to occur. Instead, it was simply the greediness that was ever prevalent in human nature that ended up becoming the undoing of all who took the pill.

A lot of people, after taking the pill, complained that they were only able to succeed once in what they wanted, and the second time, the pill wouldn't work. And what a travesty that was, to only be able to find perfection once. To still have parts of their lives that they would have to struggle through, or work to complete, or try and fix on their own. After having something like the pill bring them complete absolution once, they never wanted to have to try and fight through it a second time. They didn't want to have to try and face down their fears, or be a failure again!

Outcry rang out through the streets. This had to change, the people demanded. It simply wasn't acceptable!

Of course, the lab that developed the pill had said clearly that the pill was a one-time use only. It wouldn't work the second time, and once it was used, that was it. A single wish, which it granted. Wasn't that enough? To have something come true with virtually no effort, to have fantasy become reality? Wasn't it enough that the pills could bend the laws of physics, of time, and give these people something that was, simply put, magic condensed into a single capsule?

But the greediness of people made them want more and more.

When the pills first came out, people wished for their debts to be paid off, or for loved ones to be cured of illness. They used their wish to buy modest homes, to ensure that they would never go hungry, to make something happen for a beloved family member. People brought their family members and pets back to life, made it so their favorite animal would never die, and granted their children all the luck and happiness in the world.

And then the wishes, as they came true, as people realized what could be done with those pills, began to change. Suddenly, it wasn't health or prosperity that people wished for anymore. They wanted promotions. They wanted to master a skill without ever even attempting to learn it. They didn't want modest homes — they wanted mansions and expensive cars. They wanted people to return their affection and love, which was arguably a terrifying thought, that someone could simply wish for someone to love them, and the pills would make it so.

And so, they kept taking it. The wishes grew more and more lavish. The people, when they realized that they could only ever use the pill once, began to make more complicated and vast requests, trying to twist the rules so that they would be granted with more than just the one thing.

That was the problem that had been overlooked. People were inherently greedy. When given something like the pill, they will milk it dry. That's why there were billionaires in the world, even as people starved on the streets. That's why the neighborhoods of Mailo, Avalyn, and Soro were filled with homes that have seventeen bedrooms and twenty baths, even as others were frozen homeless on the streets and without shelter to escape harsh climates.

Carnelian City might house those who wanted to help others, but the world was no utopia. By and large, people were out for themselves. At least, enough of them were out for themselves that it began to drastically affect the usage of the pills.

The scientists who knew what would happen if the ingredients inside of the pills overworked kept silent. Not because of ignorance, but because of fear. They had been told to sell the pills with extreme care to the government, but the government didn't care. They were told to keep quiet, as their job was done, and just keep on developing and accepting their royalties.

The government didn't care for their warnings. That's why the original disclaimer had been virtually impossible to read. Hell, that's why the pills were created in the first place! To quell dissent, to calm, to appease — and most important of all, to line the pockets of those who had a hand in the production of the pills.

It was no scientific endeavor. It was no attempt to make the world a better place. If that were true, then the warnings of the scientists would have been heeded. Strict regulations would have been put down to go along with the sale of the pills. People's usage of the pills and the wishes that they made would have been monitored more closely. They couldn't care less of the possible after effects.

These after effects, mind you, were kept under wraps. No one who had worked on the project could share it, not even with their family members. It was said that one man tried to warn his sister from taking the pills, and both the scientist and every member of his family had simply vanished. Clearly, the government had absconded with them!

But... what happened? Were they put in prison, sent off to Siro, the most guarded jail on the planet? Had they been killed, put down like rabid dogs? You would have thought that the common people would speculate.

They didn't.

Only those who had known the man personally gave it any thought, and they knew better than to discuss it out loud. The government, it seemed, had ways of hearing things they should be unable to hear. Was that a new technology, a bug that had been planted near the relations and friends of anyone who worked on the team?

Perhaps.

Or perhaps, it had been the wish granted to a member of the government after taking the pill herself. Council woman, Elizabeth Montero, certainly seemed smug in her television appearances. And some thought that she appeared to have black creeping into the whites of her eyes.

"No," said her spokesperson. "It's just the bad lighting from the interview! While Elizabeth Montero fully supports the usage of the pill, she has not yet taken it herself."

A reporter questioned, "Why not? Is she leery of it?"

"No," the spokesperson said with a laugh. "Miss Montero is hardly leery! She simply wants to make sure that there's plenty for everyone else! As someone who has already made great strides toward her goals, Miss Montero prefers to leave the pills as an option for those who are struggling. Isn't that wonderful of her?"

And suddenly, all that the newspapers spoke about was how kind and wonderful Miss Elizabeth Montero was, and how kind and wonderful the government was, and the missing people were all but forgotten, even by those who had known them closely.

You see, that was something else that had changed. Someone, somewhere, must have used the pill to ensure that no journalist ever spoke about the government in poor lighting. Even the most disgusting members of the council were suddenly being praised in the various articles that covered them, highlighting how incredible even the ugliest law was going to be.

The world was changing, and not for the better. Already, within the first six months, the pills were being abused. Most didn't notice. Those who did still didn't care.

All they cared about was the chance, the way in which they could complete their dreams, and the way in which they could properly manage their ideas. They saw these pills as a solution to problems that didn't truly exist, and they were damned and determined to make use of them. They turned a blind eye to anything that was less than perfection, opting to ignore the red flags that were slowly creeping into existence around the world.

They would not say a bad thing about these pills. They simply would not!

It was one of the most important things that this world had seen, as far as development went, and everyone wanted a hand in it. People were desperate to get their goals fulfilled. They were desperate to see their dreams be brought into reality. It didn't matter what drawbacks there were. It didn't matter what risks were being taken, or how little testing had truly been done on this final project.

No one was concerned about how the government might use it to squash out rebellion and fully control the people of their country, how lawmakers could use it to get things passed, how billionaires would use it to undermine their workers even further. No one stopped to think about the oil companies that would be able to mine in the coral reefs unhindered, or the building companies that now had full access to the tropical forests.

And what about wishes and desires that warred with those of other people? What would happen when someone wished for the tropical jungle of Etalwa to be returned to its tribes, and someone else wished that their company would be able to drive those very tribes away, so that Etalwa could be used for logging and real estate instead?

No one asked that question, and the scientists were bound by contract not to give out any answers or warnings, or even so much as acknowledge that it was a risk they were not fully confident in dealing with just yet; that it was something they hadn't gotten a chance to test out in their labs before the government whisked the final product away for wholesale and distribution.

But that was fine.

It was fine, really!

The people were happy not knowing about the drawbacks to the pills. They were thrilled to be ignorant; for once, they were all far more concerned about the pleasant outcome than anything else.

Including eight particular people who had felt they had suffered enough from their lives.

Now, this was a common sentiment. It was why the pills had become so popular in the first place. The people saw a way out of their suffering — even if it was just perceived as not suffering in the same sense we would picture — and they jumped at the chance. People wanted to change their lives. They wanted to create a dream reality, where they would never again feel sorrow or discontent.

The pills gave them a means to do that. Globally, people were decrying their normal lives, using the pills to step away from the nine to five work week, from the expectations of their families, and from the failures that had haunted them. It was, simply put, a daily occurrence that someone would decide their lives would be much better if they took the pill.

It was the sole purpose of the pills to be taken so that people could forgo all of the strife and suffering in their life.

And yet, something about these eight people stood out. Their stories were… different, you could say. They were something that caught the eyes and the attention of those around them, for better or for worse.

First, was Kyra Kilmarie.

Young Kyra was, in a way, the black sheep of the family. Unlike her sisters, she didn't have the beautiful curves nor the wavy hair that they were known for. Unlike them, she didn't have the sense of fashion and the sense of appearance, and instead, she looked shabby in comparison. Where her three sisters, Leila, Lilith, and Selene were considered to be damsels, she was just a common wallflower, a little bit frumpy.

A lot bit frump, actually.

It was common to hear Mrs. Kilmarie chide Kyra at the dinner table, "Can't you at least try to put a little more care into your appearance? I know you can be beautiful if you put the effort in. Dress up, even if it's just once in a while. Darling, don't you see how much better that would be?"

Better for their social standing in the City of Avalon, that was. Mr. Kilmarie was a high-ranking official, and Mrs. Kilmarie was well known for hosting soirees and other such parties, at which her three eldest daughters were always the loveliest, in their swishing gowns and with their dazzling curls. And Kyra was always the talk in the back of the room, as people muttered about her clothing choices and the lack of effort she put into obtaining a princess-like appearance.

In fact, at the start of each soiree, before the guests began to arrive, Mrs. Kilmarie would all but beg, "Kyra, please. Just go borrow one of Leila's dresses."

"It won't fit me," argued Kyra, who was thin and lanky whereas Leila was thick and curvy. "It will look even worse on me than this. At least this fits!"

And she would gesture to whatever simple black dress she had chosen to wear for the night.

Without fail, her mother would recoil, turning up her nose and baring her teeth, much like an angry cat. "Having something baggy would be better than that. Don't you remember what Caydence said?"

"I don't care what he said," countered Kyra. "What's it matter what he thinks about me?"

"Appearances are important," Mrs. Kilmarie would retort. "If you're ever going to get married, you're going to need to put more effort into things. Just because your sisters don't have to…"

She trailed off.

Kyra knew what her mother meant, of course.

She wasn't a colorful person. She was just a normal person whom she didn't want to be. She didn't want to be normal. She didn't want to be normal because she wanted to be better than her family, better than her sisters.

Her sisters never put any effort into their appearances. They were simply born beautiful. And beauty might not have mattered in places like Carnelian City, but it most certainly mattered in the City of Avalon. Anyone could accomplish anything that they wanted in Avalon, but only if they had the appearance to go with it.

The three older daughters of the Kilmarie family had just that. Some even likened them to the goddesses of old, to the marble statues that would sometimes be dug up in Hecca and sold for millions and millions of dollars, only to decorate the halls of the rich and upper echelons.

In fact, one could find oil portraits of those three sisters in that very spot! They were often painted by locals who were captivated by their beauty, and then those paintings would be sold at auctions for obscene amounts of money. There were few politicians within the City of Avalon who did not have the portrait of a Kilmarie daughter hanging in their mansion — and there were none who had a portrait of Kyra Kilmarie.

It wasn't just the politicians who favored the three older daughters, though. Kyra knew that her parents had always favored them. But with the help of the pill — well, now it was her time to shine. It was her time to show the world how she could also be of worth, that she could also be of use to the world. Life wasn't only about beauty, and if it was, then she was going to be the most beautiful woman in the world.

And so, she took that pill, and she willed it to change her into the most beautiful woman in all of the City of Avalon. As the City of Avalon was already home to some of the most pristine beauties, this skyrocketed Kyra Kilmarie into being one of the most beautiful women in the entire world. That's why her wish was so well-known — because it was not just the manors of people in the City of Avalon who vied to have her portrait on the wall, but members of various government agents all across the world!

Even the King of Metsalla bought, not one, but three different oil paintings of Kyra Kilmarie, which he hung up in the foyer of his palace for all to see. She was featured on magazines, billboards, and television advertisements. She was a face that everyone knew.

And for a time, she loved it.

But let's not get into the times when it changed just yet. Let's take a look at the other seven players in this dangerous game.

Second, was Jessup Midat. Jessup… was done with it all. He came from a family that still thought a man had to get a job and, within a year, had to get married, and he had both of them. His wife, Eve, was a pleasant woman with luscious red hair. They lived in the Deep South, in a region known for fishing, mudding, and other outdoor activities. Jessup worked at a bait shop, and his wife frequently ran bake sales where she would sell hummingbird cakes, mudfish patties, and strips of papaya that she had candied and caramelized herself.

To many, it would have been the perfect life.

At the end of the day, Jessup was able to go home to a house that his wife kept clean, where he would eat a dinner Eve had already made — often, this was catfish or swordfish, with tropical chutneys to pair with it, and fresh herb rolls and sweet iced tea to wash it all down — and spend his evenings watching shows that he enjoyed, speaking to someone who loved him very dearly.

The only problem? He simply did not want to work. He was lazy, very lazy, and he admitted it. If Jessup had the option, he would spend all day, every day, right there on the couch watching Prism Vision, or he would spend it on a boat, fishing, far away from anyone who could ask him to do anything else.

But being lazy at work always led to his boss screaming at him, and whenever faced with a cut in his pay at the end of the month because of his laziness, it had his wife shouting at him.

See, that was Jessup's other problem. Not only was he lazy, but he was selfish. If his wife bought groceries, it was a shopping spree. If she replaced broken dishes, bought a new baking pan for the kitchen, or splurged on branded detergent, it was a shopping spree. He wanted beer kept in the fridge, but grew irate and angry any time she tried to buy herself a bottle of wine.

This only got worse when he was in trouble at work — he didn't blame his pay cuts on his own lack of ambition or his own inability to simply do his job. Instead, Jessup blamed their money troubles on poor Eve.

For once in her life, couldn't she just not have the urge to go on a shopping-spree? She could live without shopping for one month, but no, she didn't want to do that, and he had to suffer again. He had to get up every day and go into work. He had to actually put forth the effort to deal with customers and pretend to not hate his boss with every fiber of his being. And then, at the end of the day, he had to drive all the way home.

In the Deep South, as it was known, there was a single highway that connected all of the major cities with the smaller towns and settlements. That meant traffic was always horrible, especially in the late evening hours as people were leaving work. There were very few things that put Jessup in a worse mood than the fact that every day, he had to suffer through driving home on that damn main road.

He didn't want to suffer! Jessup didn't want to go into work every day. He didn't want to have to argue with his wife over lost money on his pay checks. He sure as hell didn't want to spend two and a half hours sitting in backed-up traffic five days a week.

In his eyes, he had suffered enough. He had worked enough. He wanted to rest, to simply sit around and do nothing, and even then, he would keep on getting free money so his wife, and his boss, would both be happy. Now, he had a chance to do that. He definitely was getting the pill.

Jessup was certain that it would change his life — and he was certain that getting more rest would make him a better person. One can probably imagine how well that went.

Third, was Talia. Talia, who had always been flightier than anyone else her age. Talia, who was more into the hedonistic part of life. And what was wrong with that? Talia was in her early twenties, and she thought there was nothing wrong with being in touch with her sexuality and her sensuality. She thrived on attention like that. She saw it as a boon to her own point of view. What did it matter if other people thought that she gave her body away too willingly?

It felt good!

Talia loved to go home with other people. She liked being the center of attention, she liked being focused on, and she certainly liked it when people lavished her with praise and affection. The thing that most people turned their nose up on wasn't even that Talia liked sex.

It was that Talia liked sex — but she only had romantic interest in one person.

That baffled her friends! Why would Talia go home with so many men if she had no intention of ever staying with them? They could understand having a one-night stand once in a while, but to do it every weekend, while already being romantically interested in someone?

They just couldn't wrap their heads around it — and honestly? Talia wasn't interested in trying to explain it to them. It didn't matter to her if they thought she was odd. What mattered to Talia was her own sense of worth, her own sense of fun, and her own interests.

But what about that one person whom she *was* romantically inclined toward? Well, that was complicated, too. More complicated than it probably should have been, actually. Talia was a very strong-willed girl, with very specific interests.

She wanted her best friend. She wanted him to be attracted to her, to never resist her like he always did in the past. She had it all, the beauty and the wealth, and even then, he didn't accept her advances. Talia bought him gifts, took him out to eat, and showered him with attention. She made Berthold's interests her own interests, centering ribbons of her life around this man, what he wanted, and how he viewed things.

Talia had known Berthold since childhood. They had gone to the same private school together, and then went on to live in the same neighborhood as each other. Talia had always liked him, but that like had developed into something more as she grew older.

Talia called it love. Her more aware companions called it an obsession. They could see that it had the potential to become something dangerous, long before the pills ever existed. They could tell that Talia was playing with fire, that she was walking on the blade of a knife, constantly tipping that line between being too much, too fierce, and too forceful.

It was just that Talia couldn't understand why Berthold didn't seem to return her affections! The very thought of it baffled her.

In her eyes, that was simply impossible to believe. It was impossible to believe that someone was seemingly rejecting her. How could someone turn her down; how could he reject her? That was impossible!

No one else had ever rejected Talia. She was a lovely young woman with hair white as snow and eyes that all but glittered. She had money, heaps of it — old money, actually, for her family had been some of the founders of New Celestial City, where she presently lived. Men were constantly tripping over their feet to get near her. Even when she made it clear that it was just for the sex, they would come back again, trying to get a little more of her attention, trying to spend a little more time with her.

Berthold wasn't a eunuch nor was he gay, so he had to accept her advances. Everyone else did, after all! And yet, he continued to not show the slightest of reception to whatever she did. No matter how beautiful she looked, no matter how many hints she threw at him, he just kept on ignoring her and her beauty, and she could not stand it. The longer that Talia's affections went without being returned, the more furious she became. The more furious she became, the more desperate she grew. It got to a point where Talia thought that she simply had to do something about it. Because it was getting frustrating. It was getting frustrating for her to live like this, to live without him actually responding to her.

She was desperate to change things. She craved Berthold's attention. She craved his love. There was nothing that mattered more than making him love her the same way that she loved him.

Talia would do anything to reach that end, no matter the moral qualm that others might have had about the solution that she chose. Her answer also came in the form of a pill.

And then, there was Georgina Skye.

Georgina was old. She knew it. She had lived a long, very long, life. And a very happy one, too. Georgina had spent all of her days in a small country town, which was riddled with dirt roads and people who knew each other by name. Lemkin was known for its many citrus groves, its cow farms, and the fact that there was only a single store in the whole damn town. This store was a central gathering point for those who lived in Lemkin — and that included Georgina.

Now, Georgina was not unhappy with her life, per se. She lived in a house on the same property that the Skye family had owned for nearly two hundred years. Her son, Griffith, was currently the head of the farm, running the grove, and making sure that things stayed on track. Often, when Georgina went into town to mingle at the grocery store, people would ask about him.

"How's Griffith doing?" They would question, and then Georgina would happily launch into a rambling spiel about how proud she was of her son, about how well the lemon farm was doing, and about how good her life was.

See, there was nothing that Georgina loved more than her family. Her children, her grandchildren, hell — even money! She had all that she wanted.

Georgina considered herself to be a simple woman in that way. She didn't need a diamond mine or a hover car. She just needed her family, her farm, and the local grocery store where she could stop and speak to all her friends, and where she could get all the news about the happenings in Lemkin without ever having to pick up a newspaper.

Probably for the best, as the newspaper only ever seemed to cover the pill lately. The pill and how lovely the local government was.

How strange, Georgina thought, but then again, these were very strange times indeed.

But one of the biggest problems of getting old was that she could not escape from health complications. One of those problems was Diabetes. Diabetes that she had gotten at the age of seventy for her addiction to sweets during her younger years. It seemed ridiculous to fall victim to something as small as that, something as feeble as putting the wrong thing in her mouth! Their society was so advanced, and yet, it seemed to make no difference as far as that was concerned. It seemed to be that there would never be a cure for ailments such as Diabetes — one of those things that had been swept under the rug for years.

Why? Why did her body have to fail her in a time where she didn't have to do anything but just sit and enjoy the final years of her life? Why? It just wasn't fair! Hadn't she gone through enough already?

Georgina had done her job as a matriarch. She had raised her children. She had helped raise her grandchildren. She had worked hard her entire life, always stepping forward, always making sure that she was moving in the right direction. But none of that seemed to matter.

Here she was, finally able to retire, to let others take over the business, and Georgina couldn't even do as she wanted! It was ridiculous! Insane! Absolutely uncalled for!

It wasn't as though Georgina was asking for much, either. She didn't want to travel. She didn't want to spend riches that she didn't have. Georgina's goal for retirement was simple, and one that she really didn't think should have been an issue.

She just wanted to eat sweets, and nothing else. To make it worse, her family was actually supporting those evil doctors! Those traitors!! How could they? Nope, she couldn't, wouldn't, have it. It would not end just there, and that's why, she was going to go and get the pill. So, she could finally escape the problems of Diabetes.

Kailan, on the other hand, was a greedy fellow who only wanted money. To be blunt, his entire life was about that. He was not deep. There were no layers to his story or to his personality. He didn't have some secret agenda or hidden kindness. He wasn't looking to get rich so that he could help others or pay back his parents.

No, he wanted to become the richest man in the world for his own gains and reasons! Kailan wanted a life of luxury. He wanted to be able to buy whatever he wanted, whenever he wanted. He wanted a jacuzzi. He wanted the most expensive liquors and the most expensive cuisines.

And it had simply always been that way.

Ever since he was young, he had been demanding more and more money from his parents. Not to use it, but to save it. To get more and more of it. All the money in the world, he wanted it all, and he would get it all.

He told everyone that he was poor, that he didn't have *that* much money, but he was sufficiently rich, and he didn't care about those who were struggling. The less money people thought he had, the less they would ask him for some. And he didn't want to share. The money he was amassing, it was all for himself! It wasn't for his friends. It wasn't for his family. Kailan wanted it for himself, and no one else.

As long as he could get the money, he would do whatever it took to get it. That was why he had, behind the back of his ex-wife, Clarissa, asked her parents for a dowry. They had been annoyed, but because of their daughter's happiness, they agreed to pay it.

And he didn't care. It didn't matter that this created a tension that would haunt their partnership until the day they split up. That's right — their love wasn't meant to last. It shouldn't even have existed in the first place with how Kailan viewed things, at least not on his end.

He had dumped her, in the end, and refused to return the dowry that he had been given. He didn't care about anything else, and now that he saw a way to get all the money he needed in the world, he was going to get it all. No one would be able to stop him.

And for that very reason, Clarissa had also taken the pill. Unbeknownst to him, to get revenge on him. To enact her vengeance on the man who had destroyed her, and destroy him in return. After all, she was not kind and loving, or else she would not have been attracted to Kailan in the first place. They were like two magnets, doomed to always push against each other. Only with the use of the pills, they might just finally end with one of them cracking.

Aster, finally, was prideful. Prideful about everything in the world. He saw himself as the epitome of a perfect human, as the golden standard that everyone else should follow! Aster saw himself as living perfection, as a god that had come down to Earth. There was no one else in the world who was better than him. As such, Aster didn't see why he should have to listen to others.

Why did he have to bow to someone else? His pride refused to allow him to bow. Bow to his parents. Bow to his friend who was now a member of the Parliament. Bow to his boss, he refused to do so. He had his pride, and below it, there was nothing. Aster would never give in and let someone else tell him what to do. He saw that as simply unacceptable. In fact, trying to do such a thing just might have been enough of a shock to his system that it killed him!

Pride was not everything in the world, people would say to him. But he refused to believe that. He refused to stand on a lower ground when he clearly deserved to stand higher than anyone else in the world. Sure, call him arrogant, call him a narcissist, but that was his true place in life, head held above pridefully and not kneeling to someone else. He would not bend, but his life was such that he was always forced to.

There was always someone who expected Aster to report to them. There was always someone who thought that they could tell Aster what to do, that they were better than Aster, smarter, stronger, more handsome. Well, no more.

Aster would change that. He had read the positive effects of the pill, and he was going to get it regardless of what it would, or could, do to him. For he refused to bow ever again.

And then, finally, came the one, beyond all of the others before him who wanted this pill. Do you remember him? We spoke of him earlier. We told you how his tale ended, even if we didn't say how it started.

See, that was the thing.

Humans could easily be broken down into groups. So could their reasons for taking the pill. Now, that wasn't to say that everyone took it with the same end goal in mind!

People had a lot of reasons, generally categorized under the groups of Envy, Sloth, Lust, Gluttony, Wrath, Greed, and Pride.

Do these sound familiar? They should. The seven sins of the world, all seven of these people had one particular sin about them.

Kyra and her Envy, Jessup and his Sloth, Talia and her Lust, Georgina and her Gluttony, Kailan and his Greed, Clarissa and her Wrath, and Aster and his Pride.

But some simply did not fall into any of these categories. Some were those who were beyond personal gain and wanted something entirely… more. Some, like him, simply wanted to see the world as it went on by, simply didn't want to face their own fears, simply didn't want to face what eventually was waiting for them. And yet, they had to. Why? Because that was what the eventuality was. And this pill, this one specific pill, could make sure it never happened. That was his reason for getting the pill. His reason for getting this thing that everyone was going mad behind.

He tried to reason with himself that it was not for personal gain, but deep down, he knew that he was just fooling himself. But none of them knew exactly where this one single pill would lead them.

None of them.

Chapter Four

"DAMN IT!" KYRA EXCLAIMED, slumping down on her couch in her home.

The City of Avalon was home to the cream of the crop, the top of the line of everything, and it was reflected in the lovely country estate that her family lived in.

The living room was a sign of the Kilmarie family's massive accrued wealth, which seemed to double and grow with each passing year. It had a white color scheme, with cream and gray accents. It was too bland, in Kyra's opinion — but then again, her family often didn't care about that.

She sprawled out on the overstuffed couch, slapping her head down on one of the tasseled cream pillows, and scowled up at the domed ceiling. A depiction of angels had been painted onto the ceiling, although it was also just in shades of white, cream, and gray. It was bland and hideous to look at too, and seeing it just soured Kyra's mood even further.

Once again, the day had not gone as planned. Once again, the day had failed to find her any new people who would like her. Kyra had tried! She had been as sociable as she could bring herself to be, with a focus on pleasantry in conversations the way that her mother always tried to preach about.

She had tried, and it hadn't gotten her anything at all.

Instead, they all simply flocked to her sisters, asking for their autographs.

It wasn't unusual. In fact, that was often how these days went. Her sisters would get all of the attention, and Kyra would be left standing in the background, trying hard not to scowl or cry. It was always hard to decide which was a worse outcome — and honestly, the two were often twined together.

Kyra had a horrible habit of crying when she was angry, and that often left a smudged eyeliner — which just further pushed people away from her and toward her sisters.

Sometimes, all she wanted to do was curse herself for stupidly following her sisters into their modeling business when they were clearly more beautiful than she was, and bowing down to the whims of the people who had expected her to be as beautiful as they were.

Her siblings were lovely. They were curvy and curly, with powerful strides and a way about them that made it look as if they were carved from marble. In fact, Kyra was fairly certain that at least several of the angels painted on their living room ceiling were meant to reflect the visages of her sisters.

People loved to paint them — especially Leila, who was both the oldest and the most attractive out of the four Kilmarie daughters.

In fact, Leila was the one who had started the business originally. She had been the first to go into modeling, and the rest of her siblings had followed along. Kyra had gone too, largely at their mother's insistence, but… honestly, a part of Kyra had been hoping that she would be able to prove herself as just as attractive.

She wanted to stun the world! She knew that it took her longer to get ready in the morning, and that she preferred simple, black dresses… but was that really such a bad thing? Did that truly mean there was something wrong with her? It made her unhappy to think about, that she had devoted all of this time and work to a fruitless profession.

Oh, at the start of it, Kyra had thought there was a chance. But now, the longer things stretched out, the more she was passed over in favor of her siblings.

Clearly, she was not made for this.

With a groan, Kyra covered her face with her palms. Her perfectly manicured black painted nails bit into her forehead. She thrashed about on the couch for a moment and then nearly flung herself off of it.

"I've got to distract myself," she decided, snatching up the remote for the television and flicking it on. The HD display was the best prism screen on the market. Kyra could practically see the pores on the faces of the people milling about on—

Another groan, louder this time.

"Great. It's a commercial. I fucking hate commercials."

She slumped back onto the couch, folding in on herself and throwing her arms over her chest. She huffed and snorted, and tried to focus on the commercial.

And then it changed, peeling away from cleaning products and revealing — Leila.

Leila Kilmarie appeared on the screen, showing off a line of clothing for one of the most popular stores in the City of Avalon.

Kyra was filled with the overwhelming urge to grab the remote and chuck it at the television. She wanted to see it crack into the screen and splinter, so that she didn't have to look at her sister's stupid face anymore.

A dark part of her mind pointed it out to her that there had never been any discrimination between her parents, her sisters, and herself. Whatever one got, the other would also get to use. If Leila got a new phone, Kyra would be able to use it whenever she was at home. If Lilith got a new piece of jewelry, Kyra was allowed to wear her old ones, which were equally as beautiful as her new one. It was obvious, really.

Mr. Kilmarie was very big on being fair. He loved each and every one of his daughters, so even when Mrs. Kilmarie tried to play favorites, he was there to gently steer her in a different direction. He had also tried very hard, when the four girls were younger, to make sure that they understood that they shouldn't compete with each other.

"We're a family," Mr. Kilmarie used to say. "And we need to act like it. The world out there is ruthless, girls. You need to make sure that the world between these four walls always stays good. Home should be a safe haven."

As a politician, it was very important to Mr. Kilmarie that he come home and be able to relax. He wanted his family to get along and love each other, and he always tried his best to make sure that was clear.

There was no discrimination, except in Kyra's own heart.

As she watched Leila move across the TV screen, a sour rage built up inside of Kyra. When she was younger, she looked up to Leila. She wanted to be exactly like Leila. But now, as she was older, as her fashion trends made her a less popular model, as her face was slightly dumpier than her sister's, she wanted nothing to do with her.

Instead, Kyra wanted to be better than Leila. She wanted to be better than any of her sisters.

Her father may have said that they were all loved equally, but Kyra refused to believe it. She refused to believe that she was not being discriminated against, and that she was just being envious of her sisters.

"I can't stand you," hissed Kyra to the television screen.

It clearly paid her no mind. The camera zoomed in on Leila, so she was just shown from the shoulders up. Leila pressed a hand to her mouth and then blew a kiss, winking at the audience.

"I can't stand you," said Kyra again, with more anger and bitterness soaked into the words. "I came home to get away from you, and you're still here!"

Kyra wasn't jealous. She wasn't! It was a fact that she simply refused to believe. In fact, saying that to her face was enough to send Kyra into a full-on fury!

But even if she was, well, people would understand why. After all, being the youngest sister in a group of the most beautiful elder siblings anyone had ever seen was a cause for someone be jealous of them, right?

It wasn't as though her sisters were boring. They weren't simple. They were lovely in a way that was almost ethereal. That was why they had been turned into angels on the ceiling of their living room. That was why so many senators and politicians and CEOs wanted to commission oil paintings of them to hang in their mansions.

Paintings of them. Never paintings of Kyra.

They were so beautiful she couldn't even hold a candle against them. She didn't want to be left behind; she wanted to be someone in life, too. Every day, it seemed like the gap between her success and the success of her siblings was getting larger and larger. It felt as though there was such a distance between them that Kyra would never be able to catch up.

But she couldn't help it. Her sisters were far, far more beautiful than she was. No makeup routine would ever be able to put Kyra on the same level as them, and she knew it.

Her family line was strange. Her father had blonde hair; her mother had pure red hair. Some of the people in the City of Avalon thought that they were the descendants of fae; there was simply no other way that they could have been that lovely, after all. And truly, Mrs. Kilmarie *did* seem to have just appeared from nowhere one day — Mr. Kilmarie had shown up to his parents' house, his new and unseen bride wrapped around his arm, acting like he was the luckiest and happiest man in the world.

Like the rest of their kind, all of them had lustrous pale skin and a love for colors unlike anything else that she had, or anyone who knew them had ever seen. In comparison, however, her sisters were fundamentally more beautiful than she was. Far, far more beautiful than she was.

And of course, there was the fact that Kyra… she didn't like colors. She liked blacks, blues so dark they were almost black, and maybe the occasional splash of very, very dark red. If she could go her entire life without ever having to wear colors, she would!

Her siblings didn't have that reservation, and their beauty doubled because of it.

Leila, the oldest, had sunny blonde hair like their father. So curly and beautiful, it got difficult to believe that it was hair and not fur. It was soft, so soft that someone could stroke it and keep on stroking it. She was athletic, liked to work out a lot, had a love for bright fashion, and looked gorgeous even without any makeup. In comparison to the others in the family, she was definitely the most beautiful girl anyone had seen, ever. And she was the one sister that Kyra wanted to be more beautiful than.

There was nothing in life that Leila was unable to get. It made Kyra burn with envy.

In comparison, Selene was not as beautiful as Leila, in Kyra's eyes. She had almost white hair, and the brightest smile one could find. But she didn't have the athletic beauty of Leila. She had more of a natural beauty. The natural beauty that every woman in her family was known for.

Finally, Lilith. The last of her three sisters, with ash blonde hair and an attitude to match that of a fiery rose. She was beautiful, but she was feisty with thorns. She refused to let anyone say anything about her or her family, and if someone did so in front of her, she would come down upon them with such a fury it got hard to believe anyone so small could be so vengeful. Still, she was the most caring of the sisters, which was why Kyra thought Lilith was the worst of the lot. Not because she didn't love her sisters. But because Lilith had something she never did.

Confidence.

The sisters were the talk of the street, the talk of the family, the talk of the town.

Just like now, as the commercial starring Leila finally changed, there was literally nowhere in all of the City of Avalon that hadn't been affected by them. It was as if a spell had been cast over everyone that they'd met, enchanting them, pulling them into their woven web. With their beauty, the three eldest Kilmarie sisters could get anything in life they so desired. They didn't even have to work for it.

People were constantly falling over themselves in an effort to win the favor of Lilith, Leila, and Selene.

But never Kyra.

No one ever wanted to jump at the chance to meet her, or paint her, or commission her to be their model. She was always the backup, only chosen when all three of her sisters were busy, or when the person looking to hire a model was desperate. But she was never the first choice.

Kyra was so caught up in her anger, the television seemed to phase out of existence. If anger and envy could make you ill, then that was certainly what had happened to Kyra. One might even wonder if her personality was part of why she was so much less beautiful than her sisters.

Could dark thoughts really seep out through the skin? If so, that must have surely been what happened to Kyra.

Kyra was the black sheep. The runt. The Ugly Duckling. Her family would always shout at those who called her that, but Kyra refused to care.

In fact, her family's opinion of her didn't matter at all. They were her parents — they were obligated to defend her! And her sisters were too, unless they wanted to face the wrath of their father.

She would show them. She would show them all one day. She would be standing on top of the world, and she would show them all exactly what she was made of. Kyra was pure beauty, grace, and ephemeral wonder.

If her family had fae blood in their lineage, there was no way it had skipped her! Kyra's was just buried a bit deeper. It just wasn't so openly visible.

She would show them all she wasn't the Ugly Duckling, that she wasn't the useless one, that she wasn't the one who needed additional makeup to look presentable. She had a beauty about herself as well, and she would show the world that beauty one day.

Kyra knew that, deep in her heart. It helped spur that envy into anger, and that anger into something that was only just barely shy of being all consuming hate.

She just didn't know how, because as far as she knew, there was no way to get what she wanted.

How could she change her appearance? How could she make herself grow a love for color? How could she become better than any of her sisters?

It seemed impossible.

Frustration built up in her. The commercials ended, a news broadcast starting up. At first, Kyra paid it no mind. She was getting ready to turn it off. But then the anchor said something that caught her attention.

"… and here we are giving live coverage of the store where people are lining up to get the revolutionary pill that can make your dreams come true!" the newscaster said. "I know how that sounds, but we've got the proof right here. It's been sent to us straight from the scientists who made it."

Kyra leaned forward, now interested. A pill that fulfilled your dreams? She thought it was the most ridiculous thing she'd ever heard. And yet, she found herself listening, completely enraptured by the subject matter.

"And it's no joke! This pill, in all honesty, can actually complete the dreams of people! My, what a great invention this truly is!"

Kyra took a deep breath, her eyes widening.

The newscaster continued, "The pill has only been available to the public for a week now, but we've already received reports from real people about how it has changed lives and made their dreams come true. This ground-breaking pill is meant to destroy any and all strife that you might be dealing with. I've got to say, it's something I'm really debating on getting myself! The impossible has finally become possible."

This is it! This is exactly what I need! Kyra thought excitedly, getting up and grabbing her discarded bag. *I need that pill! Once I have it... Yes, I'll be beautiful in no time! More beautiful than my sisters, and anyone else in this world!*

It was, after all, the one dream that had always been constant inside her heart, inside of her mind. It was the one constant that she had always been looking for. Being more beautiful than her sisters, being more beautiful than anyone else and gaining the praise, gaining the attention from her family.

More than anything else in the world, that was Kyra's dream. She wanted to become ephemeral. Her sisters might have been half fae, but she was going to become as beautiful as the fabled fairy queen herself! It didn't matter that it was just a children's tale — it didn't matter that there was no real proof of anything fantastical in her blood line.

Kyra was determined to become as lovely and renown as something from a fantasy story.

And if she had to take a pill, which could very well be a drug that kills her, that would allow her to do that, then she would do it. No questions asked. And she would show them all that she was worth something.

Quick as she could, Kyra hurried outside and onto the streets of the City of Avalon. She took the well-worn white paths that led to City Hall. The building itself was massive, an architectural dream. It was a large glass orb, tinted pink, with silver and white strips curving over and around it, making it appear to be a fantastical piece of jewelry that had found its home on the side of the street.

Normally, it was empty — with the old folks who would occasionally come to look over the message board out front. Today, however, a massive line had formed outside. Two city officials, clad in silver and blue robes, stood on either side of the door. Great white velvet ropes had been placed in front of it. They were only letting one person inside at a time.

That's when Kyra realized that her dreams might shatter right there on the steps, that they might run out before she could get one.

Kyra asked, "Is everyone here to get the pill?"

The woman in front of her nodded. "I'm not even sure if this is where they're selling it, but half the town seems to be here, so I figured I'd stay. Don't want to risk missing out, you know? I can practically taste it. I bet it's going to be sweet."

"Why would the pill be sweet?" Kyra asked, her brows furrowing.

"I can't imagine that something meant to make our dreams come true would be bitter," answered the woman. She laughed so hard it made her red curls bounce about on either side of her face.

Kyra said, "I suppose. I don't really care how it tastes though, just so long as it works."

The woman said, "Oh, it works. My brother-in-law already took it. Won the lottery that evening. He didn't even enter a drawing! They just rung him up with the information on picking up his check!"

"He wanted to win the lottery?"

"Since he was a kid, I guess. I don't think that's what I'll waste mine on, though." The woman gave her a wink. "Can't share that part though, darling. You know, there's an old story that says wishes won't come true if you share them. I know it's meant for eyelashes and not pills but, well, I don't think there's such a thing as being too careful."

"I suppose there isn't," said Kyra, agreeably. She didn't really want to tell a stranger what her dream was, anyway.

The line moved at a very, very slow pace. In fact, it felt like Kyra had been standing there for hours when it was finally the red-haired woman's turn. She turned to Kyra, giving the young girl a pat on the shoulder, and told her, "Best of luck, dear. Maybe we'll both get what we want before this day is done."

The velvet rope was moved. The woman went inside, and it was clicked back into place.

Kyra asked one of the men manning the rope, "Does it take long once they're in there?"

"Depends on the person," the man responded in a way that implied he wasn't interested in a conversation.

Kyra fell silent again, musing on the chance that laid before her. It seemed that after so many years of struggling and trying to get herself noticed, she was finally about to reach that goal. It was so close!

Maybe the red-haired woman was right.

Maybe the pill would be sweet.

Finally, it was Kyra's turn. The rope was removed, and she was let inside of City Hall. The inside of the building was lit with floating white orbs, which sparked with light and globules of pale yellow if anyone drew too close to them. A bright blue carpet led the way to the front desk, where a tired woman was sitting.

Kyra announced, "I'm here for the pill."

The woman sighed. Her name tag read Barbara. "Of course, you are. Alright, here. Fill out this form, and then I'll answer any questions."

Kyra took the clipboard. It was filled with a stack of papers nearly thirty pages thick. She was appalled! She had thought that, after waiting her turn in line, this would now be an easy, simple process!

There were so many steps though to get through before she was given the pill, and it wasn't that expensive, either. It was made so everyone could get it, and she could easily afford it.

It did take a couple hours for her to get it, though. The paperwork wasn't hard to fill out, but it was tedious, and it took some time for Kyra to actually work through. She took it back up to the counter and gave it to Barbara.

Barbara asked, "Do you have any questions?"

"No," said Kyra. "I don't."

"You people usually don't," Barbara touted back before getting up and vanishing into a back room.

Kyra stood there, waiting with baited breath for Barbara to return with her pill.

And finally, finally she did. Barbara came out and gave her a small red glass bottle along with a sheet of paper.

Barbara told her, "Read the instructions carefully. If you don't follow them, the pill won't work."

"I'll read them," promised Kyra.

She was so excited that she hardly thought to thank the woman before rushing out through the side door, as instructed by the large sign taped to the front of the counter.

It let out onto a bright street with very little traffic. Kyra hurried home, reading the instructions as she ran. As soon as she got home, she rushed to her room and sat down on the side of her bed. Kyra placed the sheet of paper on the mattress next to her, and then cracked open the red glass bottle and dumped the pill out onto her palm.

"Alright…" Kyra looked at the pill in her hand. It was a simple, little thing, purely white with black spots all over it. "Let's see how this goes, bottoms up!"

She took the pill, like the instructions said to do. No water, no food, just gulp it down and wait for the magic to happen. And it would take only ten minutes for her body to change, and for everything else to change as well. It scraped against her throat on the way down. It wasn't sweet or bitter. It was entirely tasteless.

And yet — Kyra was thrilled. She had been waiting her entire life for this moment, though, she had never anticipated that it would come in the form of a little pill.

She had been dreaming of this since she was a little girl. Dreaming of this particular moment, of the chance to be more beautiful than her sisters ever since she had been able to think for and about herself.

Kyra didn't just want to be as pretty as them. She wanted to be better than them, much better than them, and she would be. No longer would anyone look down upon her. No longer would anyone look at her and call her the *runt* of the four. No, she would be the alpha of the four from now on.

There would be no one else in the world as lovely as she was. Kyra thought about that dream with every ounce of her being, focusing on becoming the ethereal queen that she had always envisioned herself to be. The sort of woman who would turn heads, who would attract everyone's attention.

And that was what happened. The minute she took the pill, she knew her body was changing. She knew something was changing. A great yawning pit formed in her stomach, and then all her bones began to vibrate. It was like a mass of flies had flown into her marrow, humming and buzzing and bouncing around in there. The vibrations got worse and worse, until they were all consuming her insides. They dripped outwards, first into Kyra's muscles, and then into her skin.

The corners of her vision got foggy. For a moment, strange, black globules danced in her vision. It seemed as if there were faces in the black splotches, and in the corner of her eye, she could see something reaching for her, ghastly and twisted, a large and dark creature with sharp fangs and thorny skin, bereft of beauty, carved from the blackest of all blacks.

Kyra didn't even have time to be afraid. She blinked, just once, and both the black globules and the strange creature vanished from existence. All at once, the vibrating stopped. It's such a sudden stillness that Kyra swayed sideways and crumpled onto her mattress, as though her muscles had turned to pudding. That faded quickly enough, and strength soon returned to her limbs.

The pit inside of her stomach, strangely, did not vanish. Instead, it became much more gurgling. It became much more furious and much more interesting.

Slowly, Kyra stood up. She swayed a little, and then rushed to her cheval mirror to see if it had come true — only to be shocked by the fact that she no longer had a reflection!

"What?" Kyra reached out, pressing her fingers to the glass.

The mirror was cold beneath her hand. She could tell where her face would be, and it struck Kyra that, even without her reflection, she would be able to do her hair and makeup to perfection.

Still, it was a very odd thing.

"I don't understand why it stripped me of the chance to see myself," said Kyra. "Is it because I wanted to be beautiful to other people? I suppose… that might make sense."

Kyra wasted little time in doing her hair and makeup, letting her hands fly through the motions. It felt as if they were being guided by the hands of a phantom; someone else that could see where to swipe the mascara, where to pin the braids.

And then, when she walked out of her room, head held high, she knew the pill had worked when everyone began to stare at her. Even without being able to see herself, Kyra could tell that her dream had come true as her three sisters, who had been lounging in the living room beneath that awful angel-painted ceiling, rushed to her to gush over Kyra's appearance.

"Wow, Kyra, that's such a cool way of doing your hair! How did you manage to get it done so wavy?" Lilith cried.

"See, told you, you were beautiful, but all you wanted to do was scoff and listen to the idiots." Leila said.

Selene took hold of one of Kyra's hands and told her, "You're so lovely! I knew you would find your beauty, if you just took better care of yourself!"

All three of her sisters touted her in a backhanded way, but she didn't care. She was now better than them, than all of them.

But even then, when she looked at Lilith, she saw the woman look at her, nodding and returning back to the book she was reading. Only thing that Kyra didn't have? Lilith's way of sitting.

She couldn't sit that elegantly even if her life depended on it. In fact, out of all her siblings, only Lilith was able to sit that elegantly. It was infuriating. Even now, Lilith looked as though she were carved from marble and meant to sit on a bench out in a park for the world to gasp and gawk over. She was serenity in human flesh.

It wasn't fair; she wanted to be the better one for once. She wouldn't allow Lilith to take the limelight, not again.

Not before long, the four siblings decided that they would go out to eat. Kyra was over the moon at the chance to show the world how she was the most beautiful of them all!

This time, when they all went outside, everyone only looked at her and saw her as the beauty she was. She was proud of it. Everyone wanted to talk to her. Twice, on their way to La Luna Dosse, someone stopped Kyra, asking for her autograph. Three other people stopped and asked if Kyra was available to model for them.

It was everything that Kyra had ever wanted. She was the most beautiful of all her sisters — and Kyra was certain that she was the most beautiful in all the world.

Finally, she was achieving her dream, and so what if it cost her $2,000, she was finally achieving her dream. She was not the *runt*, not the *Ugly Duckling*, not anymore. She was beautiful. She was worth something.

She was someone who mattered.

People started to order portraits of her, great oil works that were sold to sultans and kings. City Hall itself had a picture of Kyra commissioned; it was dubbed *Fairy of Avalon*. Kyra had never been more loved by the people of her city. She had never been more popular.

Everything was perfect.

It was perfect, right?

Except… something kept pinching at the back of Kyra's head. It was like a thought that was hidden beneath layers of plaster, and someone was trying to scrape it loose with a bendable plastic spoon. Scratch, scratch, and the thought would come a little closer to the surface — but never close enough where Kyra could actually understand it.

It was like a whisper.

Like whoever — or whatever — guided her hands as she dressed for the day was trying to pass on a message.

Over the coming days, Kyra found herself getting more and more agitated. Everything about her life was suddenly on her nerves. That agitation bloomed in her chest like a poisonous flower; it welled up inside of her and spilled over the edges, like a cup left too long beneath a running tap.

"No! You aren't supposed to dress that way!" Kyra scowled at Leila, who looked at her strangely and down at her clothes. All Leila was wearing was a T-shirt and jeans, and nothing else. "It looks like shit!"

"Uh… it's a casual T-shirt and jeans I'm wearing to go on a date." Leila said. She rolled her eyes, clearly dismissing the comment.

Dismissing it!

And then the words hit Kyra. The reason for such shabby, casual wear sunk in through that fever haze of agitation and the rattling of that unknown thought.

Fire erupted in Kyra's stomach. She didn't have a date, never in her life. All of this beauty that was in her — all of the magical beauty that the pill had given her — and yet, no one had asked her out.

How was that possible? When she was the prettiest of all four sisters, how was it that Leila got to go on a date?

Kyra spat out, "What do you mean you're going on a date?"

Leila frowned, her brows furrowing. "You do remember I'm engaged, right? I've been for the past two years, Kyra, and I wear whatever I want to when I'm on a date." Then a look of understanding crossed her face, and that was somehow worse, only serving to further stir up the rage beneath Kyra's skin. Leila said, "Look, you're agitated and can't handle the lack of attention. I get it. Just go to your room until you cool off."

Kyra huffed and walked away, scowling heavily. She couldn't believe it! Leila was about to go out on a date with her fiancé, looking like that? How could Leila win someone's love when she wasn't the prettiest anymore? How could she keep someone's love when she leaves the house looking like a slob?

What was the use of the pill if she wasn't the center of attention?

Kyra stormed into her bedroom, slamming the door shut behind her with enough force that it rattled the porcelain cats sitting on her shelf. That anger grew and grew, like mold spreading over cheese, like a festering infected wound, until it was all consuming.

The only thing Kyra could think of was the fact that the pill was supposed to make her the center of everyone's world, and yet, that had not happened.

Her mother had simply praised her beauty, and then everything returned to normal. Her father looked at her strangely and shrugged, simply saying "you're still Kyra, there's no changing that, no matter how good or ugly you look."

That's not what she wanted. Kyra didn't want her ephemeral beauty to be brushed aside! She didn't want it to be written off as just a fact of life, as something that was there but not worth applauding.

The effects of the pill lasted. Everything was beautiful. For now, at least. But already, Kyra could tell that her grasp on the world's attention was slipping. Look at Leila, set to be married! That was what Kyra wanted!

Even more than that, she wanted to remain beautiful for the rest of her life. Instead, her family only focused on her for a single day, and that was it. Her parents and her siblings had only gushed over her for a few hours, long enough to go to that celebratory dinner. And then, everyone returned back to their own lives. Leila to her modeling. Selene to her studies. And Lilith to her teaching.

And Kyra was, once again, left behind. She had nothing, not even after taking the pill. Her beauty and the interest it had garnered, they were already slipping through her fingers. It was already fading — the attention shifting away from her, leaving Kyra alone. Once more, with nothing to her name, with nothing worth loving.

Or at least, that's what she thought. A part inside of her was screaming at her, screaming, shrieking at her that beauty was only ONE thing in the world, that it alone would not guarantee success in her future and her life, but she ignored it.

That thought was easily crushed beneath the anger and frustration, and beneath that itching. That awful itching at the back of her skull, like a whisper barely audible in the wind. A muttering that she couldn't quite make out but needed to.

Kyra clung to her fury.

She clung to it so tightly it hurt.

And she did not calm down.

Instead, she went out with her friend, glaring at a woman sitting at the table beside them. The woman wasn't pretty nor ugly. She wore simple clothes, but they fit her well enough. Her chest would rise and fall with every breath she was taking, and that was irritating Kyra. How could she have such rhythm in her breaths? How? How could she breathe so silently and not look as if she was panting like a dog?

The itching at the back of Kyra's skull got worse. The irritation was like acid in her veins, like it was trying to burn its way straight out of Kyra's skin.

Breath in. Breath out. Rise and fall.

"Kyra?" Her friend shook her. "What's wrong with you?"

Emma was a pretty woman, not beautiful like a goddess, but adorable enough to take home, with curly silver hair that was held back with ribbons of gold and beads of silver and white. Her dresses weren't the most expensive in the world, but they were enough to get her the attention she needed.

They had known each other for several years now, but their friendship the last few weeks had started to grow strained. Kyra didn't understand; to her, this was a fault on Emma's end. She didn't think that it had anything to do with her ever-growing pompous nature, or her increasingly tense mood, or the fact that even the smallest of things could send her spiraling off into a rant. It was making all of Kyra's relationships strained.

For a moment though, Kyra only had eyes for that woman, that woman with the perfectly rising chest, with the completely even breathing.

"That girl." Kyra scowled again. "She's breathing."

Up and down. In and out. Her breaths were perfect. It felt like there were fingers on the back of Kyra's neck, steering her toward it. Part of her mind was aware of the fact that she, herself, was no longer breathing. She couldn't match the steady rhythm of this woman's perfect breaths, so why should she bother?

Tension built up in her lungs. A slow burn filled the back of her throat, expanding into her chest. Kyra was mesmerized by this stranger, and by the way that she was breathing. Hypnotized, even.

"Uh…" Her friend's eyes rose. "Well… yeah, you know? Cause living things need to breathe, to live. Otherwise, they suffocate and die."

The reminder of breathing made Kyra pull in a sharp breath, and all that tension and burning left her in a rush. That only made Kyra more aware of how haggard and rough her own breathing was. It made Kyra even more furious with this unknown woman — and with her friend, Emma. How could Emma not understand what was going on? How could Emma not see that this was a problem?

How could Emma not be furious over it? This woman was breathing so perfectly. She was — she was infuriating. It was enough to make her want to grab a knife and throw it across the room. She wanted to do something.

"Yeah, well, she shouldn't breathe like that! I can't breathe like that! How come she doesn't look like a dog panting under the burning sun?" Kyra demanded, the pit in her stomach smoldering.

It was like when she took the pill that very first time, and the gaping pit threatened to swallow her alive. It was dark and devouring, like a pit of nothingness had opened up in her stomach, and that nothingness was trying to grow.

And she couldn't control it. She couldn't control the pit this time. She couldn't control what it wanted and what it needed because she wanted to be the best, like no one ever was. That pit wasn't just in her stomach. It was this twisting, yawning thing that spread out through her veins and seeped into her skin. It was darkness incarnate, and it was trying to control her mind. It was a one-track record stuck on repeat, and each breath that woman took only seemed to make the pit in her stomach stretch out that much wider.

Kyra needed to be the best. She needed to be perfect. That's what she told the creature that lived in the pill — the most perfect person in the world. A real-life fairy, an ethereal beauty, an eternal light in the unending darkness.

That's why she had taken the pill. No one else was allowed to be better than her! No one! But this… this random woman was better than her! How?

"Yeah, look, Kyra. You have a problem. You were jealous of your sisters, then of your family, then of me for having a blue phone instead of a red one because you suddenly started liking blue, and now, you're jealous of someone breathing." Her friend stood up, glaring at her. "Enough is enough. You know what? You're clearly not in the right mind. Control yourself, and then let's talk because this is getting ridiculous."

Emma paused, but the comment just made Kyra even worse.

Kyra demanded, "What are you doing?"

"I just told you. I'm leaving," snapped Emma. She grabbed her purse and pulled it up over her shoulder. "I can't sit here and watch you act like this. Kyra, you have to see that something's wrong. I mean, you're staring at a random woman like a psycho!"

"Wrong?" Kyra gestured at the woman with the perfectly measured, completely even breaths. "Look at that! She's absolutely perfect! How do you think she got to that point? Do you think she took the pill for it?"

"For — for breathing?" Emma stuttered. She seemed taken back for a moment, and then she just shook her head again. "You know what, this is exactly what I mean. Kyra, you can't keep focusing on everyone like this."

""Like what?"

"Obsessively," said Emma. "All you ever do is obsess over what other people have or what they're doing! It's not normal. And it's not how you used to

be. I know that you've always been a little jealous"
—

"I'm not jealous!"

"You're crazy jealous. And it's just gotten worse. I mean, listen to yourself! You're angry over how that woman is breathing? That's not normal!"

"How she's breathing isn't normal! Look at her, Emma!"

Emma shook her head. "No. I'm sorry, Kyra. I can't do this with you. Not right now. Try and sort yourself out, and then maybe, we can try and hang out again. In the meantime, I think it's best if you don't call me for a while. I hope you get better."

Better! As if there was something wrong with Kyra, and not the other way around! Like it wasn't this world that was all messed up, leaving Kyra to still struggle and try to be the best! Even after Emma's outburst, Kyra still couldn't see what was wrong.

Emma stood there a moment longer, waiting for an apology that would never come. When Kyra simply told her, "It's not my fault. I haven't done anything wrong," Emma threw her arms out to the side, rolled her eyes, and snorted.

And then she walked away. Kyra huffed, but her irritation at being abandoned during their meal quickly morphed into something else. It was that hollow pit in her gut, spreading even more as she stared at Emma's retreating form. How dare she walk away so elegantly? She couldn't walk like that, and the woman was wearing high heels, too! No, she wouldn't have that. She was meant to be the best and not everyone else! No one else! No one!

That was the whole point of taking the pill! Kyra had spent hours in line that day so she could be the best, so that she could be better than anyone else in the entire world. It was supposed to change things. Her walk should have been more elegant than Emma's. Her breaths should have been steadier than the woman currently eating butternut squash soup just two tables down. She should have been able to impress the entire world.

Kyra was meant to be the loveliest.

That itch at the back of her skull suddenly skyrocketed. It was a voice. It belonged to the creature that lived in the pill. It told her, "You were supposed to be better than them. Don't you remember? We made a deal. We made a deal so you could be better. Don't you want to make sure that you're the best in the world? Don't you want to make sure that you're the loveliest?"

Kyra did.

Kyra wanted that more than anything. She deserved to have it! She deserved to be considered the best, to be the most attractive, gorgeous, stunning human to have ever walked on this planet. Emma shouldn't be. The woman shouldn't be. None of her sisters or the other people who lived in the City of Avalon deserved to have that title.

It was only meant for Kyra!

As if moving in a dream, Kyra rose to her feet. The chair that she was sitting on scraped loudly over the ground and then toppled backwards with a crack against the tile, so loud that everyone sitting nearby turned their heads to look. Even Emma stopped, spinning around to frown at her friend.

Emma asked, "What are you doing?"

"What does it look like?" Kyra demanded.

Emma frowned. "It looks like you're making a scene! I honestly don't understand what's gotten into you, Kyra. You used to be so fun to hang out with! Now, you've become some sort of monster."

Not fun? That was infuriating, too!

The voice hissed, "Are you going to just stand there and let her call you that? Are you going to let her place others on a higher pedestal than you? The gall of it!"

The voice was right, Kyra realized. Emma really was admitting that there were other people that she would rather spend time with!

Kyra grabbed hold of the steak knife and stepped around the edge of the white cloth table. Someone screamed and jumped to his feet. A child was crying, but the sound was muted beneath the frantic, heavy whispers of the creature that lived inside the pill.

Just as it took control and guided Kyra's hands when she went to do her hair and makeup in the morning, the creature was now guiding her over to Emma.

Emma took a step backwards, looking nervous. "What are you doing?"

"Proving a point," said Kyra, ominously. And then, she declared at the top of her lungs, "Only I am meant to be the best, and not anyone else! No one else! Only me! No one else but me!"

Emma shouted, "You're acting insane, Kyra!"

Someone else shouted, "Call the police! We need help. There's something wrong with that woman. Look at her skin!"

"Hideous," someone else cried out. "Why is it turning black like that?"

Their shouts only further fueled the fire that raged beneath Kyra's skin. Because she was unable to see her reflection, Kyra had no way of knowing that an inky blackness had been spreading over her flesh for weeks. It had started at the small of her back, spreading out over the planes of her shoulder blades and curving around her sides like wispy tendrils.

She hadn't noticed as it spread down over the curve of her butt and the backs of her thighs, the shadows always hidden beneath the flowing, silk gowns, the feather-covered jackets, and the jeans made from pearls and silver chain links that she wore.

But now, as she crossed the main floor of the restaurant, her heels clacking loudly with each step, the blackness spread over the skin that was not covered by her clothing. It spread over her hands and fingers, the long, serpentine curve of her neck, and the sides of her face. The people who were around her assumed that it must have been the result of some sort of disease.

Emma tried to reason, "Put the knife down, Kyra. You're not well."

"I'm the best," said Kyra. Her words were echoed by the creature that guided her steps. "I'm the only one who matters. Not anyone else, do you understand me?"

Emma waved her hands, trying to placate the woman. "Alright, I understand. You're the best, Kyra. I know that. We all know that. Now, go ahead and put the knife down."

"Don't patronize me," she snarled, lunging forward and striking out with the steak knife. The blade cut through the strap of Emma's purse.

Emma screamed and threw herself backwards, sobbing. "Kyra!"

Other people stood up, but they weren't sure if it was safe to get involved.

Kyra announced, "You can't walk like that! You can't walk more elegantly than I can!"

She lunged again, but this time, the creature that lived in the pill guided her motions, and the blade struck true. It sunk deep into the flesh of Emma's shoulder. Bright red blood burst over the pale dress that she was wearing. Emma screamed; the sound ripped from her throat like a wounded animal.

She hit the ground. Kyra followed her, caging Emma in with her body. The knife dug into her, again and again. People screamed. Their footsteps turned into thunder as they raced from the room. Emma struggled, trying to push Kyra off.

She should have been able to do it with no problems. Kyra was a slender, elfin thing. She was not bulky or strong. But the creature that had taken over Kyra's mind? It had the strength of a thousand demons, and it held Emma still like a gravitational pull. Around them, the world seemed to warp and shimmer to some degree as the creature came further into reality and pushed at the seams of the two connecting points in the world.

Soon, Emma lied still beneath Kyra, and Kyra stared down at her friend, bloody and still. No breathing. A completely still chest, a perfect doll-like face, complete with the glazed expression of a porcelain creation.

The creature whispered, "She's still better than you. How can she be so still? You need to prove to the world that you can be more still than her."

"I can be," said Kyra.

She slowly rose up, blood dripping from her hands. As though in a trance, Kyra turned and walked over to the window. It was a large glass pane that looked out upon the city. They had been eating on the sixth floor. Kyra pressed a hand to the glass, smearing blood over it. Beneath her, the patrons of the restaurant swarmed out into the street like ants from a disturbed hill.

The creature hissed, "Prove it."

"Stop," a woman cried out, her voice trembling. She curled tighter around her child. "Please, stop!"

Kyra ignored her. Still clutching the bloody glass, Kyra turned and walked back across the room. "I can prove it. I'm better than her. I can be more still. Red looks best on me. Better than on anyone else. I'll prove it to all of you."

The next thing anyone knew, Kyra was running toward a window, and she jumped out. From the highest floor of the building. Right into the busy street below. There was a loud crash and a thump, and people screamed.

Kyra was dead on impact. The air around her body seemed to shimmer, but it was missed by most people in the panic that came from her jumping. Glass shattered onto the street, raining down upon civilians. Many of them were injured by the shards. No one noticed the fact that the color seemed to be sapped out of the air around Kyra, that as her blood pooled onto the pavement, it was a darker tone than it should be, or that the white pavement itself seemed to dull into a sodden gray beneath her corpse.

Within a week of taking the pill, Kyra had gone insane and committed suicide. Because of her envy of everyone else, because of her envy of anyone doing things slightly better than her, she had gone insane and killed herself, leaving a family filled with grief behind.

But no one attributed it to the pill. A virus, they called it. One that affected her skin. And the action itself? Well, she was simply a young woman who had cracked beneath the pressure of being a socialite in the City of Avalon. It wasn't something that many could handle, after all, and Kyra had only recently stepped into the light.

They didn't think to check and see if she had taken a pill, and while word of her spread through the city, it was simply a story of a woman who had gone mad. No warnings came out. No change was made in the distribution of the pill.

And if anyone else saw the creature that had driven Kyra to her eventual demise, it wasn't something that they were sharing.

Life carried on — for everyone but Kyra.

Chapter Five

JESSUP MIDAT HAD A GOOD LIFE, that's all he would say about it. He had managed to graduate without studying, had friends that lasted for life, and had people he could call family.

He had been born and raised in the Deep South, a section of the country that was known for its humid and searing summers, its dry and chilly winters, and the thick expanse of swamp life that seemed to be ever encroaching into the city proper. It was an interesting enough place.

Unlike some of the northern developments, like the City of Avalon, the Deep South didn't have a focus in changing the way that the Earth looked. Rather, the cities in the Deep South had decided to incorporate the swamps into their building developments. Jessup Midat lived in one such city, Archer Grove, where rather than hover cars, many of the people in Archer Grove traveled in steam boats.

These boats were designed to move quickly, efficiently, and quietly. Jessup was experienced at driving the steam boats and never had a problem getting to where he needed to go. After all, Jessup Midat had lived in Archer Grove his entire life.

His graduation, in Computer Coding, allowed him to basically work from home doing freelance gigs at his own pace and in his own space. Jessup loved it. He was able to lounge around at home, without having to fuss with styling his long mullet, or trying to find clothes that weren't wrinkled, or dealing with annoying co-workers. He set his own hours, picked the projects that he was interested in handling, and all around, considered himself to be his own boss.

Jessup was happy. He would have been content being a freelancer forever.

But his parents didn't want that. His parents wanted him to go out and get a proper job.

"Freelancing? That's not a secure lifestyle! There's no way that's sustainable! If you want to live here, then you'll have to go out there and get a *real* job. How are you going to get yourself a wife otherwise?"

That was, by far, the worst thing that he had ever heard in his life.

Margaret and Rory Midat were obsessed with the idea of having grandchildren. In fact, Jessup had been urged to find a partner ever since senior year of high school. They wanted grandchildren to dote on — and Jessup knew that they also wanted grandchildren so they could steer them toward a more traditional path in life, as opposed to the one that he had decided to take for himself.

It became a daily thing. Margaret, at breakfast, would scold, "At least put in a few applications for me, honey. That can't hurt, and you might find one you like."

Rory was much less polite about it and, at dinner, would demand to know where Jessup had applied to.

"Nowhere," Jessup would tell him.

And that would set Rory off on a rant about how immature Jessup was, and how he would never make it anywhere in life. Then the topic of marriage would come up, and the topic of children, and Jessup would eat his dinner as fast as he could manage and excuse himself from the room. He would rather sit in his bedroom all day than have to listen to them even a moment longer!

He soon got a job and quickly earned enough to move out of his parents' home and into his own apartment. Why should he have to listen to anyone if he was able to take care of himself? Just why? He would do what he wanted, whenever he wanted, for whatever reason he wanted.

Jessup liked living on his own. He painted his wall in hues of gaudy colors. He bought mismatching furniture and watched movies at three in the morning, simply because he could. There was no one around to tell him that he had to behave differently. There was no one around to try and steer his choices.

For several long months, Jessup was happier than he had been in a very, very long time. But, as everyone knows, good stories aren't filled with happiness. While Jessup was able to enjoy this life of luxury for several months, it was never meant to last.

His parents told him he'd have to get married soon. Because "that's what we want from you" and "that's what you're supposed to do." He didn't want to get married; no way in hell was he going to get married. And then he was told, quite simply, that if he refused to get married, then his father wouldn't get a promotion and may be fired from his job.

"It's not worth it, son. A life without marriage." The man shook his head sympathetically. "You need to get married, that's what men do. That's how it has always been."

And that was the end of Jessup's patience. He was done with this. He was done with this ideology.

Jessup gave in, and he reconnected with his high school sweetheart. Eve was a decent woman without any problems or drama, but the two weren't truly in love. They got married because that was the way that things went in the Deep South, and especially in small towns like Archer Grove. They both knew it was expected, and they were simply trying to make the best of it.

Things could have been worse, Jessup reasoned. It could have been like his friend Carlisle, who had to marry someone his parents picked out and arranged for him. Carlisle's wife came from a rich family in the City of Avalon, and they were looking to pocket her cash. They didn't care that her face was ugly, her personality foul, and her opinion of Carlisle was beyond lower than low.

In comparison, his wife was fairly beautiful and definitely not a gold-digger. She worked as well, but not in the way that he did. She worked as a teacher who recorded videos for online classes. That meant Eve worked from home, the same way Jessup had once done. It was… infuriating, actually. Jessup knew that he should be proud of and happy for his wife, but he just wasn't. He was incredibly jealous of her.

Eve got to work at home. She often only dressed up from the waist up, since nothing else was visible in the videos. That meant she often spent the day in comfy, slouchy pants. When she wasn't recording videos, she was able to do her other hobbies — like baking.

As far as Jessup was concerned, Eve had an amazing life. Was it really so different from his freelancing work? Jessup didn't think so. But when he tried to do the same, his parents would scream and holler at him. But when she did it?

"Wow, look at the young woman, Jessup! Isn't it fantastic that she's able to make a living for herself without even leaving the house?" It wasn't fair at all. He wasn't going to accept that.

Jessup couldn't spend his entire life listening to his parents demean his dreams. He couldn't spend his entire life watching Eve work the job that he wanted. It just wasn't something Jessup was willing to do long term.

That was why, when he agreed to get married, he accepted the transfer from the suburbs, where he lived, to the big city. His newfound wife agreed, and the two of them left their suburbs behind and moved to the big city, living in a small apartment with enough space for the two of them to do whatever they wanted to do.

The first thing that Eve did was put in a garden. Their apartment overlooked one of the many canals that wove through the city, and the sunlight would dance off the waters. Because this wasn't just some small southern town, the waters went through a treatment plant. The air didn't reek of musk and mold, or the other things that often made a bayou smell odd. It was just as clean and glistening as the waters.

Of course, in keeping with tradition, clean water didn't mean the canals were empty! In fact, they were swarming with life! Small, brightly colored fish swam through the water in massive schools. Children were able to walk over and feed them, so long as it was accredited fish food. There was a fine for putting leftovers in the water, as the city officials were leery of drawing larger fish into the canals.

"Apparently," said Eve one morning after they had just moved in, and were sitting at the table having breakfast together. "There was an incident with a bull shark about ten years back. It was truly nasty stuff, and everyone's worried it's going to happen again."

"Fascinating," said Jessup, though he didn't really mean it.

Eve, as a teacher, had a very large love for learning. She was constantly reading or asking people questions, and generally, was always trying to find something new to study. Jessup, on the other hand, was content just learning the basics of the city — which stream went where, when traffic was the worst, and where the closest coffee shop was.

Still, during that first week, things looked a little bit brighter than they had been before. It was decided that they wouldn't bother trying to paint any of the walls. Ideally, they would eventually get a larger apartment somewhere else — Eve wanted a place that would let her have a dog, and Jessup didn't want to argue with her so he went ahead and agreed.

He didn't want dogs. He hated them.

Didn't matter, anyway. It was a road that he wouldn't have to cross until later on. For now, Jessup was busy dealing with the move, unpacking, and as always, dealing with his parents.

His parents didn't approve of the move because, in their words, "There can only be one home, and the city is corrupt," but they couldn't do anything about it. It was his and Eve's decision, not theirs. Not anymore. Jessup had made the call that he wouldn't let his parents rule over his life anymore. For too long, Jessup had let them dictate his every move! Now… now, he was the only person who would have any say over his own life.

One week turned into two weeks, and then they had been living in the apartment for a solid month. Jessup liked the life he was settling into. He especially liked that there was so much distance between himself and his parents. It made things a lot easier.

He only called them once a week, and that was also usually because Eve forced him to. The calls were always brief and usually ended up putting Jessup in a sour mood. He hated them.

One day, he argued with his wife, "They're my parents, and not yours. I should get to decide if I'm going to call them or not. You just don't get it, Eve. You don't know them well enough to understand why I can't stand them."

"I understand you think they are behind the times." Eve said gently. "And I know you didn't want us to get married, even I didn't. You are a good man, Jessup, but that doesn't mean you don't have your own problems. Just don't ignore your parents."

Eve didn't have any parents of her own; they had both passed away when she was very young, and she had been raised by an aunt that was now estranged and living in Carnelian City. As such, having a good relationship with Jessup's parents was very important to her.

Jessup told her, "If you want them spoken to so much, why don't you call them yourself?"

"Because they don't want to speak with me," said Eve. "You're their son, Jessup. You're the one they want to speak with. They're your parents. You have to respect them."

"Hah!"

"I'm serious! The only reason they hassle you so much is because they know that you have a lot of potential. They want to see you do great things."

Jessup countered, "Well, I want them to leave me alone so I can live my own life."

Eve reached out, putting a hand on his shoulder. "Just try and call them more often, okay? For me?"

Jessup rolled his eyes. "Fine."

But he didn't actually mean it. Honestly, Jessup figured that his parents were lucky getting even *one* call a week. Jessup could just decide to never call them again at all. Some days, that still seemed like the option he should have gone with.

Eve might have been viewing his parents in a good light, but Jessup didn't see them that way. He knew that they didn't care about Jessup being happy or successful. They just wanted him around so they could control him.

Still, that was the only thing that Jessup and Eve fought about for a long time.

So, yeah, Eve was everything he would want in a girl, truly. She was beautiful, kind, and gentle, and she had a great attitude to go along with it as well. The one thing he didn't like, however, were her standards. She had a style of living that was sky high. She liked to go shopping every weekend. She liked to go out to fancy restaurants and appear like she was a celebrity, dressing up in makeup and jewelry, even when she was just lounging at home.

Eve was from the swamps. The backwoods neck of the Deep South. But as soon as she moved into this new and bustling city, Eve decided to try and look as though she belonged. She was constantly changing the color of her hair, getting her nails done, and trying to find the latest fashion trend. One week, she would only wear clothing that was covered in glitter, and the next, she would only wear clothing that was solid black — not a stitch of color to be seen.

Eve would do anything to be seen as high class.

It took too much work for Jessup to be even remotely interested in trying to do the same. The amount of time required to maintain that much income was ridiculous. Eve was only earning so much from her online tutorials, and most of it were wasted on her trips to the salon and mall. She may appear as if she wasn't like his parents, but she wasn't much different. Yes, she did buy the groceries, and yes, she did cook, make sure the clothes were washed, and the house was kept tidy, but his mind ignored that and simply chose to focus on one thing.

Eve liked to spend money. It didn't cross Jessup's mind that she was sweet and hard-working. He never stopped to consider that his wife maybe deserved those nice things. All that Jessup could think about was how much money they spend each day — and that led Jessup to begin thinking about how little time he had at home to do his own hobbies.

Eve kept up on the house, but she also still had plenty of time to herself. Jessup felt as though every waking moment of his day was devoted to work. Not only that, but it was a job that he hated!

Why did he have to work so hard? Why did he have to go out, every single day, sit in that office chair, listen to his boss berate him, come home, and then hear an earful from his wife because he was berated at work, and then again at the end of the month when he got a five percent pay cut? It was insane.

Every month, the same thing happened. Every month, more of Jessup's pay was taken away.

Eve asked, "Can't you try and put a little more effort into it, honey? Just for a month or two so they stop coming down on you so hard?"

"I don't tell you how to make your videos," Jessup snapped at her. "So, don't you try and tell me how to do my job. I'm excellent at it!"

He was the best in the business, even his boss admitted it, so he could get some leverage, right? Apparently not.

Eve looked upset. She sniffed and told him, "Don't raise your voice at me," and then turned and left the room.

As if she hadn't just been yelling herself! It didn't matter to Jessup that Eve hadn't actually raised her voice, or that losing money was a truly valid concern. He didn't want anyone to tell him what to do — and that included his wife.

"No, I don't care how many all-nighters you have to pull! Do you know how much is dependent on you finishing this render?" His boss yelled at him that day. "Thousands! That's how much! So, don't you dare tell me 'It's so much work; just give me some time off, and I'll do it tomorrow' because you never do it! Forget a pay raise; you'll be getting a cut this time as well!"

And that was basically what sent him to the gallows. Because when he got home, Eve was right there, with another earful.

This time, she really did raise her voice. It was the first time that he had ever truly heard Eve screech. That's right. Screeching was the only term that could be used to describe the way she was talking.

"You got a cut, again. What is wrong with you?" Eve screamed at him when she saw his monthly deposit. He was so tired of this. "Why can't you just focus for once and stop being lazy?"

"It's too much!" Jessup protested. Actually, it wasn't. All he had to do was put in an hour more, but he didn't want to. Because he wanted to laze about, watch TV, and eat snacks. "It's too much work! You wouldn't understand!"

No one understood. Jessup thought he must have been the least understood person in the world. Why was it so hard for everyone to just let him do what he wanted? Why was it so difficult for them to just let Jessup sit around and watch his shows?

"Oh, it's not too much work, you lazy idiot! It's because you just don't want to!" Eve shouted again. "I haven't gone out for a single shopping trip in over two weeks. Do you know how bad I looked when my friends and I all met up, and I couldn't even get a new dress?"

And there it was.

That was the real reason why Eve was so worked up over this. She didn't really care about the fact that Jessup wasn't happy with his job. All that his wife cared about was trying to fit in. What was the big deal, anyway? Who cared what other people thought?

Jessup sure didn't!

"You have eighteen new dresses just sitting in your fucking closet!" Jessup rolled his eyes. "And a shopping trip every weekend is too much. If you want extra money, why don't you cut down on the salon trips and add them into your stupid shopping budget instead?"

Judging by the way that Eve's face twisted into something angry and rueful, that was clearly the wrong thing to say. She slammed her hand down on the counter that she was standing next to.

"Why don't you just buckle up and be a man? You're getting cuts simply because you've given up! I've seen your speed when it comes to doing things you love, so why can't you apply the same to your job?" Eve exclaimed back. "I've had enough of this argument with you. Don't make me do this again next month because this has been going on for too long!"

And sure, it had been going on for too long. Jessup just had no interest in changing the way that he was doing things.

He didn't like fighting with his wife, but he liked having to work even less.

And that was the end of it. Eve, having said her piece, turned and stormed off toward their bedroom. The sound of the shower being turned on filled the air a moment later.

Jessup sighed, grumbling under his breath as he slouched over the couch, turning on the TV. The explosion of an action-adventure movie drowned out his wife's shower. Good. Maybe like that, he could pretend that he was the only one in the house. It seemed like that would be the only way that he was ever going to get any peace around here.

Eve just didn't understand. This wasn't fair. The fact that everyone expected so much from him just simply wasn't fair!

Why? Why did it have to be him who had to work hard? Why couldn't he just do whatever he wanted, whenever he wanted, and however he wanted? A couple more hours of sleep and relaxation won't do any harm to anyone. He simply wanted to do things at his own pace.

Why was that so difficult? Jessup knew that some people enjoyed a fast-paced lifestyle. They could find pleasure in devoting every hour of their day to working, and then crawling into bed and sleeping only to repeat it again the next day. They could be content with that. But he couldn't!

Jessup just didn't want to work. He shouldn't have to be forced to do it.

The movie went to commercial — it had a catchy jingle. The sound caught his attention, and Jessup looked up to see an ad that had never been played before. There was a woman standing at the center of the screen. She held up a bottle and said, "Is your life bringing you down? Are you filled with seemingly unending strife? I was! But then I took the pill."

A mass of script appeared at the bottom of the screen. The writing was so small, it was impossible to read, and it scrolled at a ridiculously fast pace. There was no way in hell that anyone would ever be able to actually read what it said.

The woman continued, "The pill is specially designed to make your greatest wish come true. This is a fully-backed product, created by the brightest minds in the world. All it takes is a single dose, and you'll never have to worry again."

That was it. There were no frills, no fancy special effects. It was just a woman talking about the magical benefits of a new medication. A pill to erase strife? Something that could make all his wishes come true?

Jessup's greatest wish was to never have to work again. To be able to do whatever he wanted, whenever he wanted.

So, with that mindset, when he looked at the ad of the pill being sold, he knew instantly that he was hooked. A way to get money without ever moving? Consider him sold! Jessup stood up. His wife was still in the shower. He decided that this was worth leaving the house for, right then and there. He got dressed and left Eve a note, promising to be back soon. He didn't tell Eve where he was going or what he was doing. It was selfish, but he didn't want his wife to be able to get the pill, too. He wanted to be the only one to swallow that magical little device.

Jessup rushed outside, taking the weaving canals until he could find somewhere that was selling the pills. It didn't take long before he found it. The long line of people standing outside was a dead giveaway.

He secured his spot in line and settled in to wait. And while he was just standing around, it still made Jessup very angry because he hated having to stand for an extensive period of time. He wanted to be on his comfortable couch back home, stretched out with his shoes off and his television on. This felt like one more sleight against him. Why couldn't the pills be mailed to his home instead? Plenty of products were delivered through the mail these days! He didn't see why the pill couldn't be done the same way.

It took over four hours of standing in line, going through checks, and making sure everyone knew what they were getting themselves into. It was a simple white pill with golden spots on it. He could tell because the vial that it was contained in was completely transparent. They were all scattered about in neat little piles on the back counter of the station. When he had given his reason for getting it, the man behind the counter sighed, rolled his eyes, and walked to get one of the vials.

The man passed one of his co-workers, stopping long enough to mutter, "Yup, one more lazy idiot getting a magic wish."

The two men snickered at each other. Fury filled Jessup. He wasn't a lazy idiot! All he wanted to do was sit around, do nothing, and still earn money. Was that too much to ask for? He had already done his work by going to college.

What was so bad about that? People shouldn't need to spend every moment of their day working! They should be allowed to enjoy life!

The man gave Jessup a vial, warning, "You need to make sure you're sitting down when you take it. Make sure that you read the instructions. There's a scroll of them in the bottle."

"Yeah, yeah," snapped Jessup.

He snatched the bottle, having no interest in being polite to someone who thought that he was a lazy idiot. He hurried back to the house, where he found his note tossed in the trash. Eve hadn't left a note of her own, but she was also nowhere to be seen. Even her purse was gone.

"Probably spending more of my money," grumbled Jessup.

He made sure to read the instructions, which were simple: a warning to not eat or drink anything with the pill, and to sit down before taking it.

Jessup hurried over and plopped himself down on the couch. Then he shook the single pill out onto the palm of his hand, taking a moment to marvel at it. How strange, that something so small would be able to cause such a big difference!

He popped the pill into his mouth and swallowed it dry. The powdery casing made his throat itch and scraped against his esophagus the whole way down. It hit his stomach with a plunk, instantly sending a wave of nausea through him.

The sound of whispering started up. He snapped around on the couch, twisting to stare at the door. A wave of dizziness hit him at the sudden motion. He lost his balance and fell off the couch, hitting the ground with a thud and a groan. His stomach rolled, threatening to spill its contents all over the floor.

No wonder you weren't supposed to eat with it!

The whispering got even louder. It was trying to say something, but there were so many voices overlaid on top of each other, Jessup couldn't make out the words. His vision started to go dark. Just as the world began to dim, Jessup saw someone standing at the doorway to his bedroom. For a moment, he thought that it must be his wife — Eve must have been home after all!

But then he realized that it was a large and bulky creature that wore a skin of thorns. It crossed the room and reached down, fingers stretching out toward Jessup. Just as the creature's fingers touched the front of his face, Jessup passed out.

When he woke up, the creature was gone, and he was still lying on the floor. The front door had just clicked shut, and Eve came into the room, looking unhappy.

She asked, "What are you doing down there?"

Jessup groaned and sat up.

"Are you hung over?" Eve demanded.

"I'm not hung over," snapped Jessup.

He quickly hid the bottle that the pill had come in under the couch and then stood up.

The effect of the pill was quick. He *just* took it, and already, he knew the world was changing. He could feel it. Whatever that creature had done to him, it was already sinking in. Jessup's perception of reality appeared to be altered to some degree. He felt like there was an idea brewing, something important, a half-formed thought.

Jessup brushed past his wife and went to get a shower of his own. He was exhausted. When he came out of the shower, he lied down and fell asleep in a matter of seconds.

He dreamt about the creature that lived in the pill.

Jessup didn't know where that thought came from, only that it was true. The demonic monster, all covered in black, lived in the pill. It stood in front of Jessup, and it put both hands on either side of Jessup's head. The fingers were so long that they stretched up, meeting at the top of his skull. A strange, awful coldness seeped into Jessup where their skin met.

The creature spoke to him. The words made no sense. They weren't even words, not really, just sounds. Sounds and images. And yet somehow,

Jessup understood what he was being told. He understood what it was that the creature wanted from him.

Jessup woke up with the whispering in his mind. It was almost two in the morning. Eve had joined him, lying on her side, her back to him. She was still angry over the docked pay, clearly, and over the fact that she assumed Jessup had been drinking.

He stared up at the ceiling. It was covered in thick swathes of shadows. There was a face in the shadows. He could see it. If he woke Eve up, would she be able to see it, too?

But no — that couldn't be allowed. This wasn't something to be shared. This face was his. It was a gift that the pill had given to him. It was something that Jessup deserved. He would keep it a secret, clinging to the knowledge until it no longer had a use.

Jessup had the feeling it was a secret that he would be keeping for a very, very long time.

The next day, he sat down to his laptop at work and worked hard enough to create a program that would basically complete all possible tasks that his boss would assign him. It was such an impressive program; Jessup didn't know how he did it. But the effects of it were visible starting from the very next day. Two days after he took the pill.

It was as if someone else was in control of his hands. At times, during his programming frenzy, he thought that he had caught sight of someone else in the reflection of the computer screen; someone with no face, someone holding tight onto the backs of his hands. But it was always just a fleeting thing, and Jessup quickly forgot about it in favor of typing out the next line of code, and the next one.

He knew that this was about to change his entire life. And it did! He was able to send the program to his boss that very evening, and when he went into work the next day, he was met with his boss smiling instead of yelling for the first time in months.

"Well, that's just amazing, isn't it?" His boss praised, looking at the program. "See, told you, you had it in you. You knew exactly what to do, and yet, you just decided not to. You've still got three more to do, though."

That would normally fill Jessup with dread and anger. He would wonder why the one program wasn't enough, why he still had so much more to do! Only today, that wasn't a problem.

But this time, Jessup didn't need a time frame. His program would complete the task without him even needing to move. So, all he did was sit behind his desk and wait for everything to be completed for him.

It was the best thing that ever happened to him. Sure, he had to look like he was working, but that was easy! Jessup was able to plug headphones into the computer and listen to podcasts and the radio. He scrolled online and watched videos, pretending to do work on the computer, enjoying the fact that he was basically getting paid to do absolutely nothing.

The four hours that he had spent in line at the police station, and the money that he had spent on the pill, really were paying off! Jessup had never been happier. He had never been more relaxed. And that meant when he showed up at the house that evening, there would be no fights between him and Eve.

Each day seemed to be better than the last. Jessup's good mood kept building and building. There seemed to be no downsides, no drawbacks, and no bad effects from taking the pill. It was, simply put, the best decision that he'd ever made.

During the next week, he completed his monthly quota. He met the deadline for all the projects and did something extra, without even moving. Jessup didn't know how the pill worked, actually. He didn't know how the pill operated, but it did operate, and he was able to start working from home like he'd always wanted.

"I think you deserve it," said his boss. "You're getting work done three times faster than anyone else at this company. That deserves a reward."

And so, Jessup was finally able to move his job into his home office — and it only got better from there, as his program continued to do the work for him, leaving Jessup completely void of all responsibilities. Without having to be concerned about his boss or a co-worker coming by and looking at his computer screen, Jessup was able to mess around even more! He was able to play games online, scroll through social media, and even watch videos without headphones in.

He was living the high life — and it was something that Jessup could only imagine would get better from there.

His boss was happy at the end of the week when he completed all the work without a single mistake. It was such a good thing that Jessup was called in to have his picture taken for Employee of the Month. He was seated on a stool in the break room and told to smile.

Snap! Snap!

The cameraman frowned. "Huh. That's weird."

Jessup frowned, too. "What's wrong?"

"Must be something wrong with my software," said the photographer.

He turned the computer monitor around so that Jessup could see it, revealing the pictures that had just been taken. Each one was warped, as if the very air around Jessup had been crushed like an empty aluminium soda can. There was something wrong with Jessup's face in each shot too, as if there were things pressed against the sides of them.

Jessup said, "That's not normal. I hope you don't plan on charging me for that."

The photographer asked, "Is it coming out of *your* pay check?"

"I — guess not," admitted Jessup.

What did it really matter to him if the company got scammed, anyway? It never did anything for Jessup! Always shoving work at him, and tight deadlines, forcing him to take alternative measures like the pill.

It was their own fault if they hadn't vetted out the photography company ahead of time. That wasn't Jessup's fault. He left without the photographer being able to take a single decent picture. It didn't bother him one bit. It wasn't as though he had to go into the office these days and look at it.

His wife was happy at the end of the month when his pay check was twice as much as usual, and his company was happy with how his work was attracting new clients. And all Jessup had to do was… nothing, just sit around and stare at the computer in front of him.

It was finally the life that he had always dreamt of! A small part of Jessup was disheartened that he had become so successful, and his parents would never notice, but that didn't matter too much. At the end of the day, his life was as close to being perfect as it had ever been.

And, as was often the case with people who had finally gotten their way, Jessup was too self-absorbed in his victories to truly notice that taking the pill had come at a cost. That it was changing things. That it was changing him.

He never did notice how the area around him was appearing droll, or how his pale skin, like the rest of his kind, was slowly turning gray. He didn't notice how he was getting slouchier, not wanting to do the easiest of tasks like getting up and going to the bathroom or taking a shower, the latter of which he only did because his wife told him to. In his mind, he didn't need to do anything. He didn't want to do anything, just enjoy his life as it was and ignore everything else.

The whispering was still present, but it was worse whenever Jessup had to force himself out of his chair to go and do something. He was certain the voice was trying to tell him something. It was trying to give him a message. Those bony fingers would curl around the sides of Jessup's face, trying to hold him still, to keep him on the chair.

And oh, Jessup wanted to listen to them! Doing even the most basic tasks had become too much of a challenge. Each day, he spent longer and longer in his home office, sitting on his chair. Exhaustion clung to him, but it was more than that. It was almost a physical thing, draping around Jessup like some sort of a blanket, holding him still to keep him comfortable and warm.

One night, things took a turn. Jessup was bored, and he didn't want to move at all. Eve had sent him out to pick up dinner because he hadn't left the house for an entire month, and she had become extremely annoyed at him. But he didn't want to move. Why should he move? He had spent his whole life moving; he was done.

"That's right," said the voice, finally more than just a whisper. "Stop moving. Just relax. Let it happen. Let the world exist around you. Let it take you. Let it swallow you."

That sounded pleasant to Jessup, who stopped moving right then and there.

"Hey! What are you doing? Get out of the street!" He heard someone shout.

Why would someone shout at him? He was doing everything needed of him: get a good salary, keep his wife happy, and keep his boss satisfied! What else did anyone want from him?

"Move!" came the voice again. "I can't stop in time!"

It was a young man on one of the new hover scooters that had become popular. Jessup looked at the oncoming vehicle, but still refused to take another step. And in an instant, the man on the scooter slammed straight into Jessup.

Pain shot through Jessup's side. He went sprawling out — splash! Straight into one of the canals that Eve had always found to be so beautiful. The water was warm, and it washed over him, soaking through his clothes and his skin, filling his mouth and his lungs.

There was a split second where Jessup thought to try and swim to the surface, but then the midnight fingers of the monster curled around the sides of his face, and the thought to put forth the effort to save himself left him. Instead, Jessup sunk to the bottom of the canal, where brightly-colored schools of fish swam around him, and he stayed there as water filled his lungs, and he drowned.

From a distance, people screamed and cried as the body rose to the surface of the canal. On the other side, Talia, who was leaning on her new boyfriend, scoffed and looked at her man adoringly because he was unable to refuse her. The pill truly was great.

Chapter Six

TALIA SOLACE ALWAYS KNEW that she was beautiful. Far more beautiful than anyone else, for sure. She knew that people were immediately attracted to her whenever they saw her. To say that she was vain would be an understatement. Talia looked at herself in the mirror and saw a living goddess. She walked as though the very Earth around her belonged to her, as though there was nothing else in the world that mattered nearly as much as she mattered.

What Talia wanted, Talia got.

That included men. They loved her. They adored her. When she flirted with them at the local waterside bar, they all but fell over each other trying to buy her drinks. She was constantly having, and loving, one-night stands. Talia was a woman who saw a lot of gain to be had in the pleasures of the flesh; she knew that she had a lot going for her, and she could take that and use it to her advantage.

Drinks weren't the only thing that Talia could flirt her way into. She had also been given free boat rides, free movie tickets, and even the occasional free rent. She lived her life to the absolute fullest every single day. Her body was poised and perfect, and Talia saw no reason why she shouldn't use it to her advantage.

Oh, she knew that not everyone thought the same as her. Talia had been called a slut on more than one occasion — usually by the girlfriend of someone who had gone home with Talia at the end of the night. But that just didn't matter to her.

Talia only cared about having fun, enjoying her life, and feeling good.

Well, actually, that wasn't true.

There was one other thing that Talia cared about.

See, Talia had a great time sleeping around with people… but she still had an end goal. At some point, Talia wanted to settle down and have a real family. She wanted to have the sort of life that she could enjoy and be proud of.

You know, in the future!

It was just that the one man she was attracted to never returns her advances. It was infuriating. Everyone that Talia *didn't* actually care about, they would jump at the chance to spend time with her! They would leap at it! But the one man who Talia wanted to date in earnest, he seemingly had no interest in her.

It wasn't just infuriating. It was maddening. And Berthold wasn't even a great catch. He was a simple man who lived in a simple house. He was average-looking, with average intelligence and average skills. He didn't work out much, so he was pretty lanky, and he barely made enough to support himself.

Talia, on the other hand, was beautiful, as everyone would say to her. She was everything that men loved and women hated. Blonde hair, beautiful body, and a smile more dazzling than the models shown on TV. Why would someone want to be those skanks when they could be like Talia? She was everything everyone wanted, and yet, someone no one could get because she only had eyes for Berthold, a man who never looked once in her direction when she'd try to flirt with him.

Why didn't he? Talia thought. *He was an idiot, a self-centered idiot who didn't know greatness even if it punched him in the face.*

It was frustrating. She had the most beautiful body, she knew that. Not out of arrogance, but because it was a fact. Their neighborhood had announced a beauty contest, and she had won without even trying her best. It had actually ended up being a totally boring night, because the judges took one look at Talia and knew that she would be the winner. They didn't even glance at anyone else who participated.

At the end of the contest, even the other women weren't upset. The runner-up announced that she knew competing against Talia would have meant an impossible win, and that really, the other girls had just been competing to see who would come in second place.

Everyone knew she was the most beautiful girl in their area. People adored her. Talia always wore the top-of-the-line clothing, she always did her makeup to perfection, and she made sure to eat in a way that would prevent her skin from breaking out. In fact, Talia was so gorgeous that her skin all but shone like a diamond! It was something to be proud of, for sure.

And Talia was very, very proud of her looks.

She was also very stubborn. Once Talia had made her mind up about something, she knew that there would be no changing it. She would get what she wanted, and that was that.

And everyone knew that she was heavily attracted to and borderline obsessed with Berthold. Her parents, his parents, her friends, his friends, they all knew. Because Berthold wasn't like the others. He wasn't a deviant or a jerk or a wannabe like the other boys around her. He was respectable, innocent, and pure, and she loved that. So, that was why she waited. Her mother told her that at seventeen, boys only either cared about things they shouldn't or thought that girls are objects, seeing them only as one-night stands instead of someone to form a relationship with.

Talia didn't mind being a one-night stand for most people. She thought it was fun, and often ended up leading guys on instead of the other way around. Berthold was different, though. Berthold was the one person in the world who would only ever be with a woman if he wanted to marry her.

At first, Talia was fine with waiting for Berthold to come around. It gave her a chance to have fun and mess around with other men without feeling guilty. As time passed, however, the thrill of being with other people began to lose its charm. Slowly, Talia became more focused on the fact that she just wanted to be with Berthold. She hated having to wait around for him. She never had to before. Men were always chasing her, not the other way around.

But after four years of waiting, she was getting very frustrated because he simply was not giving her the attention she wanted, needed, or deserved. He never really went out on dates. He'd spend most of his days at work before going back home to a nice home-cooked meal.

Berthold seemingly wasn't even interested in a relationship! He was so career-oriented that he didn't even notice when Talia was trying to be more than just friends. He was always polite when they spoke, but only in the way that Berthold was polite to everyone. He was just a simple guy. But in Talia's mind, he was supposed to treat her differently.

Talia didn't want his smiles or his words. She wanted his hugs and his kisses. She wanted to be close to him, closer than she had ever been. For four long years, Talia had been waiting for him. She had been hoping that he would come around of his own free will, that he would just wake up one day and realize that Talia was more important than his job, than anything else in his life.

But it seemed like no matter how much time passed by, nothing changed. Berthold was only interested in being friends with Talia.

"Just give it time; he'll get the clue." All of her girlfriends told her.

Talia listened to them at first, but then, nearing the end of the fourth year and the start of the fifth, Talia decided that she was no longer interested in waiting around. She refused to wait, not anymore.

It was during a girl's night out with her best friend that Talia came to that conclusion. She announced, "I refuse to do it anymore. I've spent years waiting for Berthold to realize what I was offering him, and he hasn't! I just can't keep up with this. I have to do something about it."

Cara slurped from her milkshake. "Okay, but like, what are you going to do? You've done everything but take your shirt off in front of him."

Talia lamented, "I know! And the problem is, I'm not sure he'd even notice if I did that!"

Cara hummed. "Yeah, you're right. He's kind of the guy to just ignore that while he pretends to politely look elsewhere."

"I don't know swhat I'm supposed to do," said Talia. "But this is driving me up the wall. There's got to be something I can do!"

A logical person might have just cut their losses. They would look at Berthold, look at the way he was behaving, and accept the fact that Berthold just wasn't interested. Some people might even wonder if Berthold swung the other way entirely!

But not Talia.

Talia was a single-minded sort of person. She saw that Berthold was the only person who could resist her charms, and it only made Talia more determined to be with him. She was borderline obsessed with it.

It might have been wise for the people in Talia's life to discourage her from continuing this futile campaign — but they weren't interested in that. Talia was so beautiful! They truly felt like she deserved to be with whoever it was that had caught her eye!

Besides, if Talia officially hooked up with someone, it meant that her friends would finally have a chance to get a man themselves when they went to bars or out to clubs on the weekends, as opposed to just sitting around while Talia took all the cute ones for herself.

Getting Talia and Berthold to finally hook up with each other seemed to have no downside for anyone.

That's when a friend suggested an idea to her.

"Hey, you know about the pill, right?" Her friend, Cara, asked. "The new one that just came out? I've seen commercials for them."

Talia nodded, face still buried inside of the tablecloth of the café. "Yeah. Of course, I've heard about them. Everyone's heard about them."

Cara said, "Then you should get one."

"Why?" Talia asked, looking at her. "It's not like I can spike his drink with it or anything."

Even Talia didn't want to go down that route. She wanted Berthold to love her — she wasn't interesting in trying to force him to. That just felt wrong to her.

"No, silly. It's not a drug! It's a life-altering pill that you can take only once for a single wish of yours to be granted." Cara giggled, eyes dancing. "I took one to be able to be the best at my job, and it works! I assure you; everyone calls me the boss now, even my own boss! You should get it, really."

Now, at this point, Talia would have noticed various things. The stress that Cara was facing. Her twitchiness and the aura around her. She would also have noticed that Cara's pale skin was already gray, and she was slowly turning dark.

Much like various others who were turning dark around her. Cara had taken the pill almost three weeks ago, and the effects were finally appearing on her body in very clear and obvious ways. It was altering her, changing the very world around her. And it was making her determined to have people listen to her.

Cara insisted, "Trust me, Talia. The pill really does work!"

Talia should have noticed the slight tremble in Cara's voice, the way that her fingers curled ever so slightly against the top of the table while she all but insisted that Talia go get a pill. She should have noticed these very odd and very alarming differences in her friend.

But she didn't. Like most of the world, she didn't notice that anything was strange about Cara — or about anyone else who had taken the pill. Or rather, she couldn't. Because the minute she heard "it works," her mind had already flashed to the number of things she could do with it.

It's difficult to call a substance that she had never taken an addiction, but that truly what these pills were.

They were creating addicts by flaunting a solution to all of that person's problems. Talia was already thinking about how a magical pill could change her entire life, and about how much better things could become for her.

Mainly? The easiness at which she could end her frustrating problem with Berthold, and make sure he was attracted to her and to no one else.

Now, some people might not have seen a difference between taking a pill to wish Berthold into loving her and spiking his drink, but Talia did. She reasoned that it was perfectly fine to use the pill, as she was the one who would be taking it.

Talia asked, "And they work?"

Cara leaned across the table. There was a mad curl to the smile that she was wearing. "They do! Talia, taking this pill will absolutely change your life. It will make your wish come true, without a doubt!"

"Where do I get this pill again?" Talia asked, her eyes glinting suddenly. "Because if this truly works, you're going to be a godsend."

"I've already told you it works," snapped Cara, finally leaning back in her seat. "Stop questioning me." She took a long slurp out of her milkshake, then smacked her lips together. "They're selling them at one of the hospital buildings. I think it's the one right near the big dock. You know, the one out by Grace Frost?"

"I know the one," said Talia with a bob of her head. "And what, you don't need to make an appointment or anything like that?"

"No way," said Cara. "And they've been out for a while. When I went, the wait time in line was almost nine hours! But I hear they're moving people in and out of the building way quicker now. They really have the process down to a science."

Talia joked, "Maybe someone wished for their job to become easier."

Cara smiled at her. "You could be right. That might explain it. So, are you going to get one, then?"

"Soon as I'm done eating," answered Talia. "If you don't mind me skipping out on our plans early."

Cara beamed at her. "Girl, I don't mind at all! Not if it means you're finally going to have your dreams come true. That's important, you know? Dreams coming true." She was drumming her fingers more insistently on top of the table now. "You're going to like what the pill does. I just know it."

Talia knew it, too. She trusted Cara. They had been friends for a very long time, and Cara never lied to her about anything before. Talia saw no reason to think why her friend would start now, especially not over something so important.

That's why Talia left the moment they finished their meal, hurrying across town so that she could get her pill.

And in just three hours, she walked out of the hospital building with the pill that she needed. It was exactly what she wanted in life, a single pill that would truly change everything in her world. The guys had looked at her like she was crazy when she said her reason, clearly wondering which dense idiot was unable to figure out that this stunning woman was attracted to him. But now? Now, she had exactly what she needed.

The pill was stored in a solid black bottle, one that was heavily shielded so the light of the storage unit wouldn't damage the pill. She had been instructed to go home and take it, and to make sure that she was sitting down during the process.

Talia didn't bother going home, opting instead to park her car at the nearest outside restaurant patio, order herself a Martini, and shook the pill out into her hand. It was white, with flecks of red and pink on it. She sniffed it, but the pill had no smell. She stuck her tongue out and licked the surface of the pill, only to recoil and make a face at the absolutely abysmal flavor.

"Disgusting! They couldn't have figured out how to make it taste better?" Talia grumbled to herself.

She didn't think that dreams should taste like someone's dirty gym socks. They should have tasted like an exquisite dessert.

But there was no changing how it tasted now.

Bracing herself, Talia swallowed the pill and then tossed back her drink, using the stringent liquor to smother the taste. Luckily, Talia had no gag reflex, and thus, didn't have to make a fool of herself for hacking and retching in public.

At least, that's what Talia originally thought… right up until the dizziness hit her, and she fell out of her chair. Talia grasped at the table cloth, trying to stop her fall, but she only managed to bring the whole thing down on top of her.

People rushed over to her aid, crowding into Talia's personal space to check and see if she was alright. Among the people crowded into her space was a dark and mysterious looming creature. It looked down on Talia and reached out for her.

She gave a choked scream, trying to scramble away, but her limbs didn't want to move. It was as though her entire body had turned into stone. The creature pressed one massive hand to Talia's chest, long fingers sinking, not just against her skin, but through it.

It felt as though the creature's fingers were curling straight around her heart!

As quickly as it happened, the creature pulled away, and Talia regained control of her limbs. She gave a single terrified scream, her eyes rolled back into her head, and she passed out.

When Talia woke up, she was in her house, on her couch, with a sticky note on her chest.

The note read: *I order you to stay put until you feel better. I don't want to be called away from work to come and get you again. Cara.*

Talia felt a bit guilty that someone had called Cara, but mostly, she was just curious about whether the pill had taken effect or not. Talia went into the bathroom, but her face looked the same. She took off her clothes, ready to hop in the shower, and stopped at the sight of her chest in the mirror.

Five black spots were sitting on her chest, right where the fingers of the creature had sunk into her. The odd thing was that the black spots were only visible in her reflection. When Talia looked down at her body, she saw only her smooth, diamond pale skin.

"That's… weird," she whispered, but decided not to spend too much time dwelling on it.

Cara said that the pill worked, and Talia trusted her. She was certain that her friend would have warned Talia about any ill effects that the pill might have come with!

And so, Talia brushed it off, took her shower, and got dressed for the evening. It was time to truly test whether the pill worked or not.

That evening, when she met Berthold, he was unable to keep his eyes away from her. He didn't know exactly what had changed today, but something had changed, and for some reason, Talia was looking more beautiful than every other day.

Talia could tell that his eyes were practically glued to her. She ran a hand through her bright pink pixie cut and tilted her head to the side. It worked! She could tell that the pill had changed something, and she was excited to see exactly how much had been changed. Those weird black spots on her chest were a great trade-off in exchange for this.

"Hey, Berthold!" Talia gave a bright grin as she hugged him. He had agreed to go out with her on a romantic dinner, and he had come to pick her up at her apartment. This was a huge step in the right direction, as Berthold normally would've just said that he was too busy with work for a night out. "How have you been?"

"Oh, you know, just dandy." He shrugged, giving her a smile. "You look beautiful."

"Really?" Talia looked down at one of her favorite dresses. A blue ruffle dress shirt and black jeans, and her smiled widened. "You think so? You've never called me beautiful before."

It was true. In fact, Berthold might have been one of the only people in the entire city to have never said something like that to Talia. Hearing it from him now — it was enough to make Talia's heart feel light and fluttery in her chest! It didn't matter that this was just because of the pill.

It was still what Talia had always wanted. The semantics behind it didn't matter. What mattered was that this was finally happening.

"I haven't, but you're always beautiful," Berthold said truthfully. "I think that all the time."

Talia cheered inside of her head. Never before had he complimented her like this, never. "That's sweet of you, Berthold. It means a lot to me, hearing something like that from you."

"That's not it. I've wanted to tell you how pretty you are for a long time. There's something else I've wanted to say, too. I just… didn't know how to say it." Berthold trailed off, giving Talia a truly adorable and utterly sheepish smile.

"Oh? Say what, Berthold?" Talia asked, shuffling closer to him so their bodies were touching. Berthold shivered at the feeling that traveled through him, but he still kept on looking deep inside of her eyes. "Say what, Berthold? You can tell me anything."

Talia wanted to hear it.

No, it was more than that. It wasn't just a want anymore. It was an all-consuming need. Just as Talia's body needed to breathe, just as she needed to eat and drink, so too, did she need to hear what Berthold had to say. It was as vital to her as living.

In fact, it might have been the only thing that would truly result in her continuing to live.

"I…" Berthold opened his mouth before closing it. Even under the influence of the pill, he was still the same bashful, deeply southern man, or so it seemed. That was endearing. "I've… I… uh… really like you. Like, really like you."

The words were like music to Talia's ears! And yet, like a succulent chocolate she wanted more of!

"Oh?" Talia asked, raising an eyebrow and wrapping her hands around his shoulders. "And?"

That wasn't enough. She needed to hear more. She needed to hear all of it.

She was, for once, glad they were standing outside of her apartment with no one else in the hallway. If he were going to confess, then she wanted to be able to finally kiss him. Each second that ticked past between now and then seemed torturous.

"I've wanted to date you ever since we were fifteen." And then it all came out. "But I couldn't ask you because I'm a nobody, and you're really beautiful and—"

And she pulled him down, their lips touching. It was a messy slide of lip on lip. Berthold's hands settled on her, one on Talia's lower back and the other on her side. His fingers bunched up in her clothing, and his lips pressed more fully to hers. Berthold's tongue flirted with her lower lip, and she opened her mouth, letting him lick his way inside.

It felt like there were even more fingers brushing over her skin, touching her cheeks, the sides of her neck, like someone was holding onto Berthold's hands and guiding them to the right spots. That should have been concerning, but it wasn't. All Talia could focus on was the fact that Berthold was finally, finally kissing her.

He pulled back, opening his mouth to tell her, "I just have always thought—"

But Talia crashed their mouths together once more, uninterested in anything that he might have had to say to her. All she wanted was to kiss him because finally, he had said exactly what she'd wanted to hear from him for years. He had said the words she'd been dreaming to hear from his mouth, and she couldn't be happier. Oh god, she couldn't be happier. This was exactly what she wanted and needed!

She took control of the kiss, pressing Berthold against the nearby wall. She angled their heads so that the kiss was deeper, sighing into his mouth. The longer they kissed, the more drunk on the sensation Talia became, and the more she knew that taking the pill had been the right choice after all.

This was the sort of thing that might never have happened otherwise. Berthold was so backwards! If what he said was true, then he had liked Talia for a while but just hadn't had the courage to admit it!

Now, some people might have wondered if Berthold really meant what he said, or if it was just the pill twisting his thoughts and turning things around.

But not her.

Talia saw this as her chance for glory, and she snatched onto it and held it close. She didn't really care how much of this was Berthold's true feelings and how much of it was just the pill. The only thing that was important to Talia was the fact that finally, she had gotten what she wanted.

And the very next day, she started her new relationship with her boyfriend. Just thinking the word was enough to make her feel giddy! She couldn't wait to start saying it out loud, to introduce Berthold to all of her friends as her boyfriend!

She couldn't believe it; all it took was a single pill, and that was it. All this time, Talia had spent moping around and lamenting about the fact that he didn't like her… and it really had been the simplest fix in the world! People popped pills all the time for lesser things. It was amazing to think that this one little pill had been such a miracle for her.

Berthold could never resist her again. Berthold could never say no to her again despite whatever she wanted to do. Cuddle in front of the TV? Of course. Hug each other until they couldn't take the heat anymore? Yup. Go out on dates? Definitely. Give me a kiss? As many as you want, Talia. She couldn't believe exactly how well this pill worked.

They advertised it as a dream come true, and that's exactly what it was. Talia's dreams were unfolding around her. Each day, Berthold met her with a smile, a hug, and a kiss. Talia was constantly asking him to come over and inviting him to go out. She was always looking for more reasons to spend time with him.

It felt like her life was finally slotting into place!

But she couldn't see how it was affecting her. Her thoughts, as always, were centered around Berthold. One day, she felt his touch on her back while he was applying sunscreen. His apartment complex had a roof-top swimming pool. It wasn't very large, but the sun caught on the surface of the chlorinated water and made the whole pool glitter like diamonds. A few fake potted plants were scattered throughout, along with several beach chairs that had seen better days.

It wasn't anything fancy, but the fact that she was there with Berthold turned it into something incredible. Talia thought she could come up here every day and never get tired of it. And look! Now, she actually had that chance!

Her building's built-in AC system was broken, and he told her to come and live with him. She instantly agreed, and there they were. It had only happened today — her bags and boxes were still sitting in his apartment unpacked, but knowing that she was living with the love of her life instead of alone was the best feeling in the world.

Never again would Talia have to say goodbye to Berthold. Never again would she have to retreat into her own quiet, empty apartment. Losing the AC unit might have been one of the best things to ever happen to Talia. Well, next to hearing about the pill, that was!

And so, they settled down beside the pool, close enough to the water that Talia's feet could press into it. The warm pool water lapped at the sides of her ankles, the sun baking down against it and against her own skin. They should have already gotten into the water, but the minute she felt his hands on her back, she knew she wasn't going to be able to move.

That was ideal for Talia. In fact, she could have happily stayed there all day!

Pleased with the contact of skin on skin, Talia twisted around so she could wrap her arms around Berthold. His hands settled around her waist, giving her a quick squeeze, and then letting go.

Talia stayed put. If anything, she held onto him even tighter, turning her head and letting it rest on his shoulder. The scent of chlorine from the pool was so strong that she couldn't catch even a single whiff of Berthold's after shave, which was a shame.

All the same, she made a happy, content sound and leaned against him more fully.

"I called you here for a swim," Berthold spoke down to his girlfriend.

She rolled her eyes and kept on hugging him, her swimsuit clad body hugging his.

"We can get in later," assured Talia.

Berthold asked, "Are you sure?"

"I am," said Talia. "I just want you to hold me."

There was an odd look on Berthold's face as though he wanted to say something. Then the skin around his eyes shifted, like invisible fingers were tugging at it, and he told her, "Alright, Talia. Whatever you want to do. I just want you to be happy."

Talia gave a loving, content sigh. She clung to him tighter, and they stood there longer. The sun baked down on their skin. But Talia was content. She couldn't bear the thought of him letting go. They sat there until the sun set, and the moon came out. Only then did they go inside — reluctantly, on Talia's end. A part of her thought it would have been more romantic if they stayed outside under the stars all night.

And this was not the end of it. Her sheer… need to do certain things soon got too much to handle. They had a cat named Petra. A little, furry cat that liked strokes. Berthold was out on a night shift one day, and Talia had been stroking Petra's fur. And she kept on going, and going, and going until Petra had enough and started to bite her.

The fangs sunk deep into Talia's hand. She yelped, jerking backwards. The cat hissed at her, got up, and vanished! Blood welled up on Talia's skin. Muttering and cursing out their cat, she rushed to a nearby sink and washed her hand. The bite wasn't bad, but it peeved her all the same.

She was enjoying spending time with her cat. It had been fun for her! Now that Petra was gone, Talia found herself feeling itchy and uncertain. Talia needed something to do.

Trying to get rid of that restless feeling, she went to the bathroom. She didn't stop to look at the marks on her chest or her reflection — which was good, for she would not have liked what she saw. The marks were spreading, turning her skin even darker, pulling away from her chest and spreading out over her breasts, feathering over her clavicle.

She got into the shower and started to wash her hair. Talia stood in the shower and scrubbed her hair until her hands began aching, and then she scrubbed it even longer until the shower rattled and stopped pumping out heat. The cold water was enough to shock Talia out of the haze that she had fallen into, and she got out of the shower, got dressed, and drifted toward her bedroom.

As soon as she was not doing something, the restless feeling came back. She tossed and turned that night, unable to settle. On the rare chance that she could actually fall asleep, she had odd dreams about a demonic creature. This creature was cloaked in black and shadows. It was saying something to Talia, but she was too far away to hear it.

She would try to run toward the creature, so that she could hear what it was saying. It felt important to understand what this odd spirit wanted from her... but Talia would always wake up before she got close enough to know.

And it didn't just end there, with petting cats and extra-long showers. Talia had an obsession. She had something that had gone terribly wrong inside of her brain. It was one thing to have an urge to do something. But Talia couldn't control herself. If she thought about it, she had to do it… and she had to keep doing it! Stopping anything became an impossible task. It was like part of her brain had snapped, and now she was stuck in this almost unending loop of craving more, and more, and more.

She didn't know what had gotten inside of her, but something had happened, and she couldn't control it, at all. She couldn't control this feeling deep inside her heart that told her to constantly move. She needed to do something, and she couldn't just do it once. It was an urge that refused to stop no matter how much she tried.

And with each passing hour, the urge grew stronger and stronger, until it was all consuming. It was like there was a darkness inside of her.

"You need it. You want it. You need it. You want it."

That's what the creature in her dream had been saying. Talia realized it with a startling clarity after waking up in the middle of the night.

"I need it. I want it," she whispered as though in a daze.

Berthold, who was sleeping next to her, reached out. Groggily, he asked, "Are you okay?"

"I'm fine," Talia responded. "I'm… perfectly fine."

And she was. That darkness had finally seeped out, filling her up from the inside out. She understood what she wanted, and she understood how to get it. And what she wanted — well, a girl like Talia deserved to have!

The next morning, this problem became deadly. All she did was drink a single cup of coffee. And she needed more. She needed more and more cups of coffee. She didn't stop at one. She didn't stop at two. She didn't stop at ten. She just kept on drinking until her body became jittery.

A strange feeling swept through her. It was like her bones were vibrating. They bounced around in her skin, rattling around, making her ache. The taste of coffee had gone from sweet to bitter. She used all the French vanilla creamer in the house and started in on the gallon of milk. Without any sweetener left, the flavor of the coffee grew worse. And yet, Talia found that it didn't matter.

She wasn't drinking because she wanted it to taste good. She wasn't even looking to get a caffeine boost or more pep in her step. It was like there was something else guiding her hand.

It was still early in the morning. Berthold finally walked into the kitchen. "Pour me a cup of that, will you?"

"No," said Talia, shortly. "It's mine."

"Seriously?" Berthold frowned. He then caught sight of the used coffee filters on the counter and the empty creamer bottle. Concern dripped into his voice, "What are you doing? I don't think you should have that much coffee, Talia. It's not good for you."

Talia poured herself another cup. "Don't tell me what to do, Berthold. Can't you see? I want it! I need it!"

"It's coffee," he told her, moving to press a hand against her shoulder. "Holy shit! You're shaking! Talia, I really think you need to stop drinking. You're making yourself sick!"

Talia did feel queasy, but that didn't matter. It wasn't up to her, not anymore. This was a life-or-death situation. She had to keep drinking. She just had to!

"Don't, Berthold, don't scream at me like that! Can't you see I need it? I can't exist without it like I can't exist without you! What is happening? Why is everything getting darker? Berthold? What the hell is happening to me?"

"Talia!" Berthold grabbed her shoulders right as her legs gave out.

Pain welled up in her heart. Talia felt ill. Even as the sickness swept through her, she was still blindly grasping for the next cup of coffee. That awful voice was still scratching at the inside of her skull, "I want it. I need it. I want it. I need it."

Tears ran down her face. "Please," she sobbed. "Please!"

She meant, "please give me another cup," but Berthold misunderstood her. He leaned down, pressing his lips to her forehead and promising, "I won't leave you, Talia. I promise, I won't leave you."

The last thing that Talia saw was Berthold's crying face, and nothing else. She had died of caffeine poisoning.

The grief that slammed into Berthold was like nothing he had ever felt before.

Two weeks had passed since then, and Berthold was alone. His life was suffering because even though he had not taken the pill, Talia's greatest wish in life was to have what she wanted. He had been forced to love her through the magic of the pill, and now, she was gone. He was in love with her, though he never really felt attracted to her, and he was bound to love her forever whether he wanted to or not.

It was like being caught up in the waves of the ocean. The tides surrounded him, pulling him under. They threatened to drown him at every turn. Each day seemed harder to get through than the last. Each hour that passed seemed to drag out for an eternity. Without Talia in his life, there was no joy left for Berthold to find. There was nothing that he could do to replace the aching spot that the pill had cut into his heart.

And he couldn't handle it. He couldn't handle a life without Talia; he was meant to be with her, and her alone. No one else. No one. So, without even hesitating, he used the knife in his hands to carve a simple slit on his wrist. His last thoughts were, *Talia, I'm coming to you.*

It was the crying of the cat that alerted the neighbors two days later. Petra was re-homed. Berthold was put into the ground.

And for the rest of the world, life went on.

In a home not too far away, Georgina Skye noticed that her skin was getting darker, but she didn't care. Her Diabetes was gone, and she could eat whatever sweets she wanted. That might not have seemed like much to most people, but it meant the absolute world to Georgina. She lived in a city called Arcadia, which had a very large agricultural base. The people loved to farm, and they often had farmers markets. These open-air markets were filled with the greatest things!

Homemade sweets! Organic honey! Pickled and candied fruits and vegetables! Rubs full of sugar, and perfect for putting on meats at the next family cook out! You see, to Georgina, food was the greatest pleasure someone could have in life, next to family. She had a very large family, and she loved her family very much… but Georgina had devoted her entire life to them, to other people, to people who could continue to live and have their own lives!

Now that Georgina was growing older and older, she decided that she wanted to focus on her other passion: sweets. Specifically, Georgina Skye wanted to focus on the fact that she loved candy. Due to her health problems, it had taken a pill for her to be able to do that.

Because Arcadia was a rural city, it had taken a while for Georgina to get a hold of the pill than it had been for anyone else. But as soon as they came to Arcadia, she snatched up a pill as fast as she could, and wished to be able to eat as many sweets as she wanted without any consequences.

She should have already seen the news. About how the pills had a serious adverse effect. But it was already too late for her.

It was turning out to be too late for a lot of people.

Chapter Seven

DIABETES WAS A PAIN. And Georgina Skye really, really did not like living with it. Her life had started seventy-eight years ago in a simple house in the middle of a town she didn't think would ever turn into a city. She didn't know what made it a city, or what changed it into a city, but she had been a little girl with big dreams that she didn't think were going to come true.

Arcadia was a simple place, filled with simple folk. They liked to grow their own food, make their own furniture, and help out others where help was needed. It was nothing fancy. Arcadia was not meant to be an earth-shattering city, and none of the people living there were destined to change the world. It was simply Arcadia. The people there were simply ordinary, everyday people.

Don't get her wrong. She had a decent childhood. When she was young, education was not as readily available, and if someone had a high school diploma, they didn't need anything else to get a great-paying job. The skills that someone needed to learn would come from experience, and that was how she had become an ice cream maker at one of the biggest parlors in town. Marguerite's Ice Cream.

It was a cute place. At first, Georgina had only taken the job because, like all people her age, she needed more money coming in per month. However, she quickly realized that working could actually be fun, if the right circumstances were met. And she loved her job. Especially because she couldn't get enough of the smells that were inside the kitchen. She couldn't get enough of the sheer taste of ice cream flavors that she was able to taste test every day.

Georgina had the strongest sweet tooth out of anyone else in her family. Hell, she had the strongest sweet tooth out of anyone who had ever lived in

Arcadia! If Georgina could have eaten dessert for every meal, then it would have made her a happy camper.

People would tell her, "Don't eat sweets, or your teeth will rot!" But that was idiotic. Who could live without eating sweets? That was the most insane thing that she had ever heard in her entire life.

Now, Georgina did try to follow the rules. She made herself brush her teeth after every meal, even if that meal was just a chocolate bar. She did have an apple once a week — although, it was normally a caramel apple or a baked apple pie.

It still has fruit in it, and that's what counts, Georgina thought.

And she was still active. Georgina loved working outdoors. She even had a nice farm, which she had hopes of eventually passing on to her future grandchildren and their grandchildren. Georgina was extremely hard-working and respectable. She just had a slight addiction to sugar.

It was a love that some thought would fade with age, but that never happened. Even after her teenage years were long behind her, Georgina still found herself a fan of anything sweet and sugary. In fact, it got *worse* with age, as she was suddenly in charge of all her own meals. Without any parents around to make sure that she was eating a more balanced diet, she found herself free to toss sugar on anything that she wanted. And oh, she loved to experiment!

Georgina would take normally savory dishes, and she would play around with them, messing with them until she could figure out whether a bit of molasses added into the sauce would make it taste better, if a bit of cocoa powder and chocolate could tighten up the flavors of a dish. Sometimes, she would even do things like put sweetener on her pizza, just because she loved the way that sweet cheese tasted!

It wasn't just food, either. Sweet tea was the only thing that Georgina Skye was really willing to drink during the day. At night, she would make herself large mugs of hot chocolate, which she topped with pillows of smooth whipped cream and colorful rainbow sprinkles. Sometimes, she would even fix herself more than just the one mug! And if she had coffee, it was always filled to the brim with flavored simple syrups until it was so sickly sweet that it was less about drinking coffee and more about drinking sugar in liquid form.

As far as Georgina was concerned, that really *was* the only decent way to drink coffee. She couldn't understand why anyone would want to drink it black. It was far too bitter for her! And why pass up on any sort of a vessel that would put more whipped cream inside of her? No, no, super sweet decked-out cups of coffee were the only way to go!

Time passed, and while life changed for Georgina, her love of sweets never wavered.

When she got married, she found the answer in the form of her husband, who was the owner of a nearby dairy. She had met him when he came to Marguerite's and struck a deal with the owners to send him wholesale boxes of ice cream to sell. They had an instant connection and soon got married.

It was a fairy tale wedding. Carlisle was a handsome man. He loved Georgina with his whole heart. Neither had any plans on moving out of Arcadia, and they both wanted to have a large family. Not only that, but they loved the same things! There was no better way for them to spend a day together than go out to an open-air market.

Their home was soon filled with handmade quilts and hand-painted signs. Plants were growing on window sills, and a large garden was put out back. Their pantry was filled with the wares of other people who lived in Arcadia, and they both took delight in selling their creations at the open-air markets.

In fact, there was only one thing that Carlisle and Georgina ever fought over. That, of course, was her eating habits. Or, more specifically, it was her love for sweets.

"If you eat too much, you'll get Diabetes."

It seemed like such an asinine comment! Over the years, Georgina had many people say that she had an unhealthy obsession with sweets. They told her that she should have a more varied diet. If she liked sugar so much, she should at least try switching over to artificial sweeteners. And oh, Georgina would never deny an option without trying it once. The problem was, she hated the taste of artificial sweeteners, especially in her drinks.

The aspartame just didn't taste right when it was put into her sweet tea. It made everything seem like it was caked in chemicals. Sugar was a natural product. Georgina was certain that it was better than the chemicals in those pink and yellow packets. She definitely thought it tasted better.

"There's no difference in the taste," Carlisle would argue. "It's not healthy for you to keep eating like this, Georgina. You're not a child anymore. All this sugar is going to catch up with you. I only say this because I love you. I want you to have a long and healthy life with me. You can see that, right?"

"I know you love me," said Georgina, but she would agree with nothing else that came out of Carlisle's mouth.

She didn't believe him when he said that. She didn't believe any of it and continued to live her life like she had been living. It had done no harm to her so far. She continued to make sure to always brush her teeth, and she never got a single cavity. She saw no reason in changing things now when she was already so far into her life. What's the point of leaving sweets? All she did was eat a single box of ice cream after every meal, and some chocolates here and there.

Georgina liked the way she ate. She liked the way that her life had played out so far. Carlisle was a good man, and she was certain that he had her best interest at heart, but the bottom line was that Georgina refused to change. This way of eating was working fine for her.

It wasn't as though it was a new way of eating, either. She had been doing so ever since she was twenty!

And so, despite the fact that Carlisle begged her day in and day out to eat just a few less sweets, she never changed her ways. She kept eating exactly the way that she wanted to.

So, one day, after a meal, she complained of dizziness after eating a single scoop of ice cream, and her son-in-law, who was a doctor himself, instantly got concerned.

"I'm fine," said Georgina, trying to brush him off.

Her son-in-law, Matt, insisted, "I need to check your heart rate. You could be sick. It can be the start of something much bigger than just a simple headache."

Feeling faint and a little itchy, Georgina sat down heavily on one of the chairs. The whole family had come over for dinner, and she didn't like feeling like such a spectacle! Just as she and Carlisle had dreamt, they had a very large family. Just then, everyone's eyes were focused straight on Georgina. She hated it!

Matt pulled a machine out of his bag, along with a small pen, and pricked her finger to check her blood on the machine, and simply said one thing.

"Yeah, your blood sugar is off the charts," he said instantly. "I can't be sure without a fasting test, but I'm pretty sure you have Diabetes."

A hush fell over the room. It felt like someone had just dumped a bucket of cold water on Georgina. A shudder laced up and down her spine, and she shook her head. "Impossible! You can't really tell from just a single blood drop!"

"Well, I can take a pretty good guess. Like I said, I would like to do a fasting test," said Matt. "But honestly, I'm pretty sure about my diagnosis. I don't think there's too much more it could be outside of Diabetes."

She refused to listen. She also didn't want to look at the rightfully victorious look her husband had. He had warned her, every single week ever since she married him, to keep control of how much she ate, to control how much ice cream she ate, to make sure she didn't screw up her future because of her addiction. And because of it, she now suffered, suffered because all of that was now taken away.

Just the thought of it made Georgina feel ill. She couldn't understand why such a disease would even exist without a cure! Was anyone even *trying* to look for a way to solve this problem?

Dinner ended quickly, and Georgina retired to her bedroom. She could hear Carlisle downstairs, cleaning up the dishes and muttering that he told her so. It was a good idea for him to give her some space, anyway. Georgina didn't want to see her husband, or anyone who would rub it in her face.

All she wanted to do was lie on her bed and sulk in the sorry turn that her life had taken. And that was exactly what she did. Georgina draped herself over the mattress, placing one arm over her face so she didn't have to look up and confront the fact that the world didn't in fact exist to benefit her.

It seemed like the cruelest thing that could have happened to her, as if life itself had turned against her. The world was not fair. She knew that. Georgina had been sick before. Her parents had grown old and passed away. She kept up with the news and knew what the world was like in other places, where people didn't rally around to help each other out. And yet, nothing that Georgina had ever encountered seemed to be as all-consuming and awful as this moment. Nothing seemed to compare to knowing that sugar and sweets were now a danger to her wellbeing.

Why? What was the point of living such a life? Without being able to enjoy the true gift of the gods?

Sweets were the only thing that truly gave her joy. All her life, Georgina had made the right calls. She had done what was best for her family, her farm, and even her neighbors. This seemed like the one thing that had always been hers; something that no one would ever be able to take away.

And yet, with this diagnosis, she could feel it drifting out of her fingers. The whole she-bang, just slipping away!

A sound from the kitchen caught her attention. Was that plastic being ripped open? It was!

Georgina finally sat up. She scrubbed the tears away from her face, and then pulled herself out of bed. She took a moment to try and righten herself, so she didn't look like a mess, and then she stepped out into the hallway, and then into the kitchen...

where she was met with possibly the worst sight in the world!

Her husband was standing in front of the trashcan, ripping open all her packages of chocolate and then emptying them into the trash bin! The ice cream boxes had been pulled out of the freezer and set onto the counter, some of them already so melted that the cream was seeping through the cardboard and onto the surface of the counter.

"No!" Georgina growled at her husband as he threw away everything in the house that had sugar.

Just the sight of it was enough to fill her with white hot rage. She didn't think that she'd ever been so furious with Carlisle in her life. She ran forward, trying to grab one of the candy packets out of his hands, wrenching it away from him.

But Carlisle was taller and stronger. He tugged it back, holding it up above their heads so that she couldn't reach it. He didn't look smug. He just looked angry, and maybe a little bit sad.

"You will not eat them, not again. You have Diabetes, Gina! You can't just do what you want!"

"It's my body! If I still want to eat candy, I should damn well be able to!" Georgina snarled.

Her husband countered, "If you want to put yourself straight into the grave. Georgina, I don't want to lose you. Why is that so hard for you to understand? This is a big deal! Diabetes is dangerous. Think about how bad you felt today, and how much worse it could get! I don't know what I would do if you died."

"I'm not going to die," said Georgina, dismissively.

Carlisle insisted, "If you don't start watching what you're eating, you will. This isn't something that can just be ignored. I want you to go and take a real test. The one that Matt mentioned earlier. We'll discuss things more after that."

Georgina grumbled and walked away, not able to do anything but watch as Carlisle dragged the trashcan out into the yard.

The very next day, she went to a doctor — but, not wanting her husband to influence the test, she went outside of Arcadia and had a stranger run her test. Much to her fury and despair, the test still came back just as her son-in-law had predicted.

She had a very advanced form of Diabetes. She would need to start taking insulin, and she needed to change how she was eating right away. This only furthered her husband's goal of removing all the sugar in the house. The fridge, the freezer, and all the cabinets were completely emptied out. Even the coffee creamer was exchanged for sugar-free, and they bought sweetener packets instead of allowing Georgina to dump six spoonsful of sugar into each cup of coffee.

Everything she loved to eat was stripped out of the kitchen, container by container, until she was left with nothing but health food and sugar-free replicas. It felt like the end of the world. There wasn't anything that she could do about it, however. Carlisle was determined to throw it all out and make sure that the kitchen was completely sugar-free.

But Georgina had a secret. She had a secret chocolate stash where she stored bags and bars of chocolate. Georgina knew he would throw them away if he found out, but she failed to take her nosy grandson into account.

Georgina had snagged a candy bar out from her stash and stood out back near the chicken coop, trying to eat it before anyone caught her. The chocolate was rich and creamy, the nuts inside of it adding in the perfect crunch and spark of salty goodness. It wasn't a very large bar, but it was enough to give her a bit of relief before having to go back in.

The whole family had come over for dinner. Georgina had found that without sugar as a coping mechanism, it was much harder to deal with them.

She was also very angry that they all seemed to side with Carlisle instead of with her; they all agreed that she needed to have a sugar-free diet.

Because of that, she had to stoop to eating outside and burying the candy wrappers where no one would find them.

Suddenly, she heard a crunch behind her. She turned around and realized that the chicken coop wasn't as safe as she had originally thought.

"Hey, Mom!" Shylo, her eldest grandson, looked at a frozen Georgina, who was nibbling on a bar of chocolate. "Granny is eating chocolate again!"

He said it so intensely, as if this was a big deal! They didn't understand. This was no different than the fact that her daughter, Tabitha, smoked! It was no different than the fact that her husband liked a shot of whiskey with his dinner!

It certainly was no different than Shylo wanting to get more pocket change so he could get something sweet to eat while he was out with his friends. Out of all her grandchildren, she had truly thought that Shylo would have understood! But there he was, turning her in.

"Mom," he called out even louder. "Mom, did you hear me? Granny's eating chocolate again!"

"Little traitor!" Georgina gnarled out, even as her daughter came rushing out the back door.

Tabitha took one look at Georgina, flung her arms to the side, and then turned back to go inside. "Dad! Dad, I need your help. Mom's still got chocolate hidden somewhere!"

Somehow, the brat knew exactly where her chocolate stash was hidden, and they threw everything out. From the kisses to the crunch bars, every last little piece of sugary goodness was thrown in the trash. They were all unhappy with her. Carlisle was so angry, in fact, that he went a whole hour without speaking to Georgina.

As if he was the one who was being betrayed.

She wasn't allowed any sweets, any at all except for the sugar-free ones. Those were disgusting!!! They didn't have the sweetness that she wanted! None of it!

They didn't taste good. They tasted like chemicals. It was practically the same as feeding her bleach, Georgina tried to argue. But no one listened to her. Everyone only had one thing to say to her. "It is for your own good. This is the best thing for you, Georgina. It's better to do it this way, we promise."

She would be the one to decide what was better for, no one else! She wanted sweets, and she was determined to have it!

Georgina was miserable, and she became even more miserable when Carlisle grew sick. It was cancer, and his battle with the disease was both short and silent. He was fine one day. The next, he was being carted to the hospital in an ambulance and given a very, very poor diagnosis. They gave him three months to live, but he only made it three weeks.

Her husband passed away, and she couldn't take it. Her life-long companion, just gone. Georgina went home that night, and she stepped into a house that was dark and quiet. There was no one to speak to, no one to watch television with, no one to hold her close at night and love. The house just felt… cold.

Georgina walked through the home as though she was in a trance. She ended up outside of the door to their bedroom, only to realize that she couldn't bring herself to go in. This wasn't just her room. This had been *their* room. Her husband for nearly forty years was supposed to get in that bed with her, and they would fall asleep the same way that they always did: curled up together, holding each other close.

Instead, the room was empty. If she went in there, she would have to get into that bed alone. She would have to sit there in the silence and in the cold with no one to curl up with. The thought filled her with too much grief. It was like a pit that had opened up in her stomach, threatening to swallow her alive. It was like — like there was nothing good left in this entire house.

Tears flooding her eyes and spilling down her cheeks, Georgina turned away from the bedroom and hurried back into the living room. She slept on the couch that night, and she dreamt about her husband, ice cream, and sitting out in the back field together like they used to.

But when Georgina woke up, she was distraught to find it hadn't just been a nightmare. Carlisle really was gone, and she would be expected to start making arrangements for his funeral soon.

And her sweets, taken away from her because of Diabetes. She couldn't handle it. She couldn't handle it at all. She couldn't live without sweets, not again. Not when she was also alone in this house, when she didn't even have Carlisle to give her safety and comfort. She wasn't certain that it was worth it.

And there was something else to think about.

With Carlisle gone, who was she really trying to live for? Oh, she had her children and her grandchildren. She even had a great-grandchild on the way! It wasn't as though Georgina wanted to die, and she wasn't considering offing herself. But she did come to the decision that the only reason she had given up the sweets was for Carlisle.

With him gone, there was no reason for her to continue being abstinent from them. Without him there to remind her of all the reasons she shouldn't be eating them, well, what was the point?

That was why, when she read in the newspaper about a revolutionary pill being sold everywhere, she instantly jumped at the chance to get one.

Supposedly, this was a pill that had been created specifically to destroy strife, the worst illnesses that the world has ever seen. While many stated that it was a pill of science, and that it had been created in a lab after many years of trials, others simply called it a "magic pill," and they said that it could do anything.

Her greatest wish in the world. Whatever it happened to be, this pill was able to grant it. It would change her life — and she only had to take it once. It had a fairly high price tag. But then again, having her greatest dream come true was worth a few grand, according to the general consensus. People loved the idea of it. Georgina loved the idea of it. She thought this might be enough to change things, to finally allow her to break out of the funk that she had been in since Carlisle passed away.

She ignored the part that said all those who had the pill had eventually gone mad and started killing themselves, and the strange disaster that had started up somewhere in Europe. There was no concrete proof to any of it, after all. It was just a lot of speculation. People making guesses, trying to come up with an explanation to everything.

Sure, a lot of the people who had gone mad had also taken the pill. In fact, all of them had. And while the situation in Europe was being kept under lock and key, there were mutterings that it had to do with the pill, too. A wish gone wrong that had started the downfall of an entire nation.

It was just… well, Georgina wasn't willing to acknowledge any of that. In fact, she completely refused to read about any of the bad things that were going on. They didn't matter. They might not even have been true! And if they were, well, Georgina thought that the risk might have been worth it. She would do just about anything if it meant that she could have something good in her life again.

All this time, Georgina had been miserable. Her life had started to go downhill after getting the diagnosis about being diabetic. And after Carlisle passed away, it had just gotten even worse. None of her family members were enough to break her out of the funk that she had fallen into. But this? Oh, this was something that might really help her! It could give her the lift that she so desperately needed, so that Georgina could once again enjoy both life and the world around her.

Georgina made up her mind. She was going to do it. She was going to take the pill.

The very next day, she got her pill. The men at the pharmacy had simply taken her application, sighed at the request, and handed her a pill. It was strange, though, that they had grayer, darker skin. She didn't know why their pale glowing skin was slowly darkening, but she didn't care.

"Thank you," she told the men because she had been raised with manners.

The men didn't say thank you in return, which Georgina found to be quite rude. She huffed, turned on her heel, and headed outside. It was a lovely day out, but… well, there was something strange going on. Certain places seemed to be darker. Rather, certain people seemed to be standing in shadows.

Georgina's gaze drifted up to the sky, searching for the thick clouds that might have been responsible, but she found none. It was a concern that was quickly brushed aside. After all, Georgina had just gotten her pill! She was finally able to have her lifelong dream come true!

Just as she had been instructed, she found a bench to sit down on. She then pulled the bottle out of her bag and looked at the pill. It was small and filled with little rainbow specks. They reminded Georgina of the rainbow jimmies that she used to order on ice cream. The thought made her mouth begin to salivate. She would soon be able to have ice cream again!

With a deep breath, she popped the pill into her mouth and swallowed it dry. Instantly, a bitter tang flooded her tongue. The curve of her throat burned. She could practically feel the pill sliding all the way down, where it settled in her gut. A wave of dizziness crashed into her, like when her sugar levels got too high. She pressed a hand to her face.

Now, this was a small town where everyone knew everyone. A kind young man named Davide rushed over.

He asked, "Are you alright?"

"Fine, fine," she croaked. "I've just taken the pill, that's all."

A look of understanding crossed his face. "I took that pill a few days back. This will pass quickly enough. I'll let anyone who stops by know that you'll be fine in an hour or so."

"An hour," echoed Georgina, but the words didn't really mean anything to her.

She narrowed her eyes at Davide, but the world was starting to go spotty. Everything blurred, until there was only one sharp spot of clear vision remaining.

It was behind Davide, several yards away. There was a creature with sharp fangs and thorny skin. Its hands were as dark as ink, and its fingers very long. It reached out, as though it was trying to grab hold of Georgina. That pit of grief in her stomach suddenly ripped open, and she began to sob. She sobbed and sobbed, desperate for something good to come back into her life.

The creature began to talk. Was that English? It must have been, but the words were so odd. They seemed too quiet to make out, even though they were too loud to ignore. They rattled inside of Georgina's skull like they were trying to brand themselves into her brain.

It made every part of her throb and ache. It made her want to scream, but all she did was cry even harder. The creature hadn't moved, but Georgina could feel a hand curl against one of her cheeks, cupping it lovingly.

The whispering got worse. It filled up the pit on the inside of her stomach and made everything throb. And then, just as suddenly as it had appeared, it vanished. Georgina found herself still sitting on the bench, Davide at her side playing on his phone. Judging by the fact that the street lights had come on, and the sun had started to set, she had been there for several hours.

Davide looked over when she groaned and smiled. "You're back with us. It's a bit of a trip, isn't it?"

"What just happened?"

It felt like she hadn't been able to drink anything in years. Georgina smacked her chapped lips together. Her tongue was very, very dry. Her lips stuck to the front of her teeth.

"I'm not really sure. Most people call it a 'Trance.' My best guess is that it's how the pill figures out what it is you really want." Davide stood up, reaching out and giving her a clap on the shoulder. "Let me tell you this, Mrs. Skye, that pill is absolutely worth it. You won't regret taking it."

"It works?"

"It absolutely does. But listen, I've got to get going, alright?"

They said their goodbyes, passing pleasantries onto each other's respective family members. Then they went their separate ways. Up and walking again, Georgina was surprised to find that she felt great! She could only assume that the pill had worked, and she instantly went to the nearest ice cream stand, where she could buy some of her favorite flavors. She had been away from her sweets for far too long. Far too long. She didn't want to be away from them any longer. Not again. Never again.

This might have been the best thing that could have ever happened to her! Georgina was thrilled at the chance to finally eat ice cream again. And not just ice cream, but hot chocolate, and sprinkles, and whipped cream, and even candy bars! All of the things that Georgina had been denied over the years, they were finally right there for her once more, ripe for the picking!

She decided that no matter what happened after this, it was no doubt the best decision of her life. Well, the second-best decision. The first best decision was still agreeing to marry Carlisle all those years ago. Nothing could truly compete with true love... or at least, that's what she told herself.

Really, one would wonder why it was candy that she had asked the pill for instead of her dead husband. One would wonder why her greatest wish was to eat ice cream again rather than to have someone else to go home to at the end of the day.

Georgina didn't wonder. In fact, bringing Carlisle back from the dead had never even crossed her mind. From the very first moment that she'd heard about the pill, she had known that it was meant for

the candy and chocolate that now filled her arms —
and would soon also fill her belly.

It was just what the pill had been meant for.

"Mom!" her daughter screamed at her when she
came to her home to check in on her.

Tabitha was so startled that her purse slipped
from her grip, landing on the floor with a solid thud.

And she saw what she had feared. Georgina.
Eating a pack of chocolates with two discarded ice
cream boxes around her. Georgina had come home
and promptly started to gorge herself. She had a lot
of years of not being allowed to eat sweets to make
up for!

Tabitha shrieked, "What are you doing? What
have you done? Matt, come quick!"

"Relax, sweetie." Georgina rolled her eyes. "I've
got the miracle medicine. I no longer have Diabetes.
In fact, I don't think I can ever get it again."

It was a simple thing. In fact, Georgina was
surprised that neither of them had ever heard of the
pill. It certainly wasn't being kept under wraps; if
someone as old and out of touch from reality as
Georgina had been able to find out about it, they
should've been able to, also.

"That's impossible," Matt, her son-in-law, said, instantly taking the empty wrapper away from her hands and pulling out the machine and pen. "There is no cure to Diabetes, and unless you found a shady doctor who made you believe that there was a cure, you can't be cured of it. I..."

He blinked suddenly, looking at the machine strangely, and then at a smug, gleeful Georgina. Then he blinked back down at the machine and shook his head. He took another test.

The same result.

He tried another part of her body, from her toe.

The same result.

It kept coming back negative, saying that her sugar levels were perfectly fine. Relief bloomed inside of Georgina. She could feel that her body had changed. That pit in her stomach, it hadn't gone away. It was a bit of an uncomfortable thing to have, a dark pit in her gut, one that seemed to be formed from grief, shadows, and sharp scraping bones, but it was a perfectly fine trade off if it meant being able to eat whatever candies, sweets, and ice cream she wanted.

"Try as much as you want, dear!" Georgina giggled, literally giggled. "I've taken the pill. I'm cured of Diabetes."

She didn't even try to keep the joy out of her voice. She didn't try to keep the smugness from her voice, either. Hah! This would show them! They thought that they knew what was best for Georgina, but they were wrong! It was her body. It was her life. And only *she* knew what the best decision for her life was.

There had been no better choice than taking that pill. She was absolutely one hundred percent certain of it.

"It is… unbelievable to think or say that you are actually cured of it," Matt said slowly. "But how? There's literally no difference in your blood sugar! What pill did you take? And why didn't you consult anyone about it first? You can't just run around swallowing random pills."

He shook his head, but all that Georgina could do was laugh even louder. It went from a giggle to a chuckle, and then into full-blown hysterics. Ask? As though anyone in her life had ever been helpful to her! As though they were actively trying to keep her away from what she loved.

She got to her feet, moving to fetch the article. It was sitting on the kitchen table in the middle of a pile of candy wrappers and empty ice cream tins. She had to brush cookie crumbs off of it — but it was fine. The article was protected by both glass and wood, so it could never get messed up.

"The miracle pill, of course." Georgina said, showing him the framed article that had changed her life for the better.

As soon as she had come home, after eating a full sleeve of chocolate chip cookies, she took the article and put it in a frame.

That evening, Georgina had plans to hang it up in the living room, above the fireplace. This article had saved her, stealing away the dreariness that her life had become and giving her hope again. It gave her joy again — something Georgina had thought would never again be felt.

She gave Matt the framed article. "See? This pill allows someone to do anything they want! I heard people can get rich, can get whatever wealth they want, can get whatever job they want, if they have this pill. It's amazing!"

Matt's brows furrowed as he looked over the article. He was starting to prematurely bald, and the worried look made him seem twice his age.

Fretfully, Tabitha asked, "Matt? What does it say?"

"I…" Matt shook his head and looked over at his very worried wife. "Don't think this is a good idea. Really. It says here that this pill is having a strange side effect, and people should stop taking it. Why the government is even selling this…"

That got a bark of laughter out of Georgina, though it was filled with derision instead of humor. "Government? Who said it was from the government? I got this at the pharmacy!"

Georgina rolled her eyes. As though she would ever take something that was being handed out by the government. How stupid did they think she was? She had gone old, not senile! She was filled with grief, not stupidity!

Matt paled even more at that. He gave her back the frame and then told his wife, "I think we should head out. We have that appointment for Shylo this evening. I know you wanted to pop in and say hello, but I don't think we should be late."

Tabitha looked confused for a moment, and then understanding settled on her face. She nodded her head, saying, "Mom, we'll be back tomorrow, alright? Just… call me if you need anything?"

"I will," acknowledge Georgina, but she knew that there was nothing she would need from them.

Everything that Georgina could possibly want had been spread out on the table. She saw the two out of the house and then went to fetch herself another pack of cookies, which she crushed into crumbs and then dumped on top of her next bowl of ice cream.

This was going to be the absolute best night that she'd had in years!

The very next day, the entire family all gathered together and questioned Georgina about the pill that she had taken. All the while, she was eating a bowl of yogurt.

It wasn't just a bowl of yogurt, of course. It had been piled full with candied fruit, Maraschino cherries, and topped off with chocolate sauce. It was the best breakfast that Georgina had eaten in years! The whole time she shoveled it into her mouth, her family stared at her. She assumed they must have been in awe over the pill's effects.

As they questioned her about the pill, it became clear that they didn't think it had been a smart decision to take it. They kept bringing up the side effects that were supposedly going around. She told them that Davide had seemed perfectly fine when they met outside of the pharmacy that day, but it didn't seem to make them feel any better.

She didn't care about their worries. All her worries were gone. This was the best decision that she had made in years! Georgina figured that even if there were side effects, they were worth it. Being able to eat whatever she wanted again was worth just about anything.

But to humor them, she allowed them to give her a blood test every morning. There was never any change. None at all. Her blood sugar stayed right where it was supposed to be, and she could eat her desserts exactly like she wanted to eat them.

And oh, she did eat them! Georgina was able to indulge even more now than she had in the past! It felt as though her stomach was never full. That pit inside of her grew and grew, and she became more and more determined to drown it out by eating as much as she could, by devouring everything in sight. Her pantries and cupboards were soon filled with nothing but snack cakes and other pastries.

She had no reason to try and eat a balanced diet now — though she did still make sure to brush her teeth after every meal. It was actually something of a joke to her! She could never get Diabetes again, but cavities were still a possibility! Because of that, she also had lots and lots of toothpaste sitting around!

For Georgina, it was as though her life had finally taken an upswing. She thought that there was surely nothing bad that could happen to her now that this was the most perfect her life had ever been.

Georgina only had eyes for her sweets.

But everyone could notice the changes on her. Her glowing pale skin was slowly getting darker and darker. Her eyes were losing their glow and becoming black pools of obsessive nothingness, and her agitation from whenever someone would take her sweets away from her was over the top.

She had been cranky over it at first, griping that she had gone so long without having them that she shouldn't have to share or give them up. But that griping quickly got worse and worse, expanding into something else. It wasn't just irritation anymore; it became explosive anger. It got to the point where if one of her grandchildren asked her for a piece of chocolate, she would explode on them, shouting at them to never touch her chocolates ever again.

Her grandchildren quickly grew to dislike going to visit her, and they began to find reasons to avoid seeing Georgina. She didn't seem to notice at all. Georgina was so focused on eating enough sweets to make up for her several years without sugar that it was just about all she did! Every meal was coated with sugar. Thick stacks of syrup-covered pancakes. Piles of waffles caked in powdered sugar and honey butter. Cakes to go with every meal!

Yogurt covered in candied fruit. Ice cream topped with sprinkles and butterscotch syrup. The list went on and on! Even things like her milk were mixed with sugary treats like chocolate syrup, so that every single thing that went into Georgina's mouth was loaded with sugar. It very quickly went past the point of being extreme.

That yawning pit had to be filled, but nothing she ate could seem to fill it. The whispering still rattled around in her skull, but now and again, she would be able to catch a word or two that came in clear: EAT, the word stuck on a repeating loop. She couldn't resist listening to it, and so she began to try and eat more and more every day. She had to fill up that pit!

Georgina refused to share with anyone, for fear of having none left if she did.

Matt, the doctor in the household, knew that they would have to do something, and soon. He began reaching out to everyone in the area, trying to get more information on this so-called miracle pill. He found out that Davide had taken it… and killed his family and then himself.

In other parts of the world, someone had gone on a rampage at a movie theater. People were stepping out in front of traffic. They were drowning themselves, slitting their own wrists, and throwing themselves off of buildings.

And no one was doing anything about it!

Matt realized that if he wanted to help Georgina, he would have to figure out how to do it himself… but it was too late.

Georgina had consumed so much sugar, and so many sweets, her blood sugar wasn't being affected. But her blood pressure was. It was a known fact that sugar provided energy, and then caused a crash. Too much sugar and then a sudden crash could be fatal.

This was not something that Georgina had considered. She had been so focused on the level of sugar in her blood that it never crossed her mind to be concerned about anything else outside of cavities. Her blood pressure got so high, blood erupted from her mouth, her eyes, her nose, and she gave a loud cry as she collapsed to the ground.

There was no one else home. The rest of her family had left after Georgina yelled at Shylo for trying to use chocolate syrup in his milk. It should not have been an issue; Georgina had three gallons of the sickly-sweet brown syrup! She just didn't want to share any of it.

So, they all left, and now, Georgina was lying on the floor by herself.

The phone was right there in front of her. Her hand extended to call 911, but then she spotted the toffees that were on her desk, right beside the phone, and she extended an arm to grab them. She knew that she couldn't move, that she couldn't breathe. She was in trouble, and she needed medical help, instantly.

EAT. EAT. EAT. It was playing on a loop in her head. The demonic creature was standing on the other side of the room. It was staring at her, its fangs grinning at her. It reached out, gently pushing the toffees closer to her.

Georgina knew that this was going to kill her. She just knew it! But her glutton for sweets simply wouldn't stop. So, she continued to eat more, and more, and more. The dark figure continued to push the treats closer to her. "EAT. EAT. EAT," came the whispering on the inside of her skull.

That pit in her gut was still open and empty. Georgina was consumed with the idea of filling it, with using sweets to finally get that last little bit of peace that she had always craved. She had to fill the pit. She had to EAT.

She didn't stop until she could no longer move. There was a pressure in her head that had built up the moment she had collapsed. A weight that she couldn't get rid of. And with each bite of toffee she took, the weight got more and more until it just snapped. Her body jerked around, unable to do anything but thrash and flail.

"EAT. EAT. EAT," said the monstrous creature.

Just as it had at the very start of this, the creature reached out and pressed its hand to the side of her face. It was cold to the touch. Then it vanished, and Georgina was left alone… but not for long!

She heard the door open, with a loud shriek and the sound of people rushing in. But she didn't care. She needed sweets. More sweets. All of them! She didn't need anything else! Give her the sweets! Give her all the sweets!

She struggled and thrashed. Her body grew weaker. She knew that her family was there, but she could not comprehend where they were or what they were doing. It didn't matter in the end.

The last thing that Georgina thought was: EAT. EAT. EAT.

And so, Georgina passed away with a stroke and a heart attack in front of all her children and grandchildren, her skin completely darkened and already affecting the area around her. The darkness on her skin devoured all the light in the air near her. It was as though she was trying to get rid of all the goodness in the world, sucking it straight into her skin the same way that she had sucked up her gummy worms.

When the government took to the media two months later to stop people from taking the pill, showcasing the photo of Georgina, no one cared to stop. By that point, word about how positively they could change their lives had spread. No one felt that the risks outweighed the gain.

Especially not Kailan.

Chapter Eight

POVERTY WAS A PLAGUE. To everyone. It was a complete terror to all who lived in this world, simply because poverty rendered so much potential uselessness that it got difficult to explain how bad it could get. People joked that money couldn't buy happiness, but the simple fact was… it could.

Money prevented strife. Money could keep your electricity on. It could keep a house over your head and food in your fridge. If you were ill, money could buy you medicine and items that would make your life more convenient, like hand rails to go inside your shower or wheel chairs. It could allow you to support your ageing parents or your younger siblings.

Money could buy the things that would make you happy. Being poor and living in poverty would only add further stress to your life. It would only make the dark days seem that much darker. When you didn't know where your next meal was coming from, how could you find happiness? When you didn't know if you would be able to make the next car payment or cover your rent, how could you see joy in any part of your life?

The simple fact was that you couldn't.

Without money, there truly was no way to be fully happy. That was a lesson that some people needed to learn the hard way.

Kailan had always loathed poverty. He had been four years old when he saw his father scream at a beggar in a foreign country they had visited, telling him to go away and stop asking people for money, that he didn't deserve to have money. His father had explained to him how bad poverty was, and that no one deserved to be poor.

At the time, it had seemed like a very strange conversation. Kailan thought that if his father hated poverty so much, and thought it was something that no one deserved to struggle with, why had he not given the man money? No amount of trying to ask about that had gotten him an answer that made sense.

Eventually, Kailan's father told him, "You'll understand it better once you are older, son," and the conversation had come to an end.

Kailan was much older now. And… well… he still couldn't figure out why his father was defending himself for shouting at a poor beggar by explaining what poverty was. It seemed like a nonsensical way to go about things, and it made him believe that his father might have been a hypocrite. But he did understand one thing.

If someone was poor, then they wouldn't get a chance to do anything in this world. They would forever be stuck inside of a never-ending trap of misery, never being able to get out of the cycle that they would always be fighting against.

There would be no pursuing higher education. There would be no exploring other cultures. If you were born into poverty, then the chances were very high that you would stay there. And the longer you stayed there, the less happiness would be found in your life.

When you were poor, the best that you could do was struggle to survive.

That was all that they would be able to do, and that was all that would happen to them. Poverty was a disease, a complete and utter disease, and Kailan refused to be poor. He *refused* to be poor and become the kid in the back of the class who everyone teased. That was not his destiny.

In fact, the very thought of it terrified him.

Now, many people were afraid of losing their homes or cars, or having some tragedy strike them that would leave them in a bind — temporarily or otherwise. It was a perfectly rational concern to have. But Kailan took it to an extreme. It wasn't just a concern for him; it was almost a phobia. His fear of being poor was so over the top that he acted insane about it.

The first pay check he got, he hid from everyone. His parents and his friends. Kailan told no one that he had gotten paid; he told no one what he made. Instead, he told them how he was being unfairly treated at work, and how some of the "bullies" that worked with him took almost everything away from him. The fact that it was known to happen thoroughly made them understand that yes, he was facing serious issues.

They lived in a bad area, after all. People were cruel, and they were cheap. They could often take things without ever being willing to give it back.

They saw how absolutely devastated Kailan was, and they figured that it must have been the truth. As a result, they decided that they would have to do something about it, to help Kailan get back what he had lost so that he could still support himself. He got the exact amount refunded to him by his parents and friends, all the while, he had his pay check still in his pocket. And that was just the start of his greed.

As soon as Kailan realized that he could get away with it, he began trying to find more ways to get money. Now, Kailan was smart. Or rather, you might be better off saying that he was incredibly devious. Because there was nothing in the world that he feared more than poverty, there was also nothing in the world that Kailan was not willing to do to avoid it. He had no problem lying to those he loved to get more money and, in fact, he often did exactly that.

Whenever he worked on projects, he would cry out and say that he didn't get enough money. Kailan was a natural-born story teller, and he was always able to weave up a good reason for why he was coming up short on expenses that week. Why someone else would need to step in and cover for him.

Kailan developed a false world around himself in which he was a constant victim.

Kailan insisted that he was always the one casted aside, and he was the one who would suffer for everyone else. He was "bullied" as he would call himself, and he needed the extra cash, any of it that he could find.

This went on for years, and no one had ever been any wiser about it. After all, they could see no reason why Kailan would be lying! After all, it was not as though he wore expensive clothing or drove luxury cars. He was not rolling in riches — at least, not that anyone else could see.

Over the years, Kailan had, using that trick, gotten about eight different bonuses meant for other people. He knew that it was wrong, horribly wrong, but he didn't care. They didn't understand his sheer fear of poverty.

It was something that Kailan had sworn would never happen. He would never let himself reach a state of being where he could not afford to pay his bills or buy himself food. So, he kept on stealing and saving every chance that he got. Even when he had more than enough money to last him for years.

It didn't matter. To Kailan, there was always a risk of being poor. There was always a chance of things going wrong. What if he got fired one day? What if inflation skyrocketed, and he didn't have enough to buy groceries? Kailan was obsessed with the idea of never letting himself go broke.

That's why, during work in late October, his boss' most recent announcement sat so poorly with him.

"Alright, we've decided that this Christmas, we will donate our bonuses to charity." His boss said, coming into the room.

The words made Kailan's blood run cold. He waited for his boss to start laughing, hoping it was a joke, but the man didn't. He was completely serious about it! A sour expression washed over his face. Donate? Charity? Like hell. He was *not* going to give away his money to anyone.

Just the thought of doing such a thing made Kailan feel terribly ill.

His boss looked over the room and asked, "Does anyone have a problem with this?"

Everyone shook their heads. Everyone, but Kailan. He knew how to play along. He knew exactly how to swindle out of giving away his share, and then some. He wasn't going to let his hard-earned, *his*, money fly away like this.

This was going to be his biggest trial yet. He'd never faced something like this before… but Kailan knew that he was an excellent story teller. He knew that if he played his cards right, he would never have to give away a single penny ever again!

So, he came up with his sob story. Right there on the spot, Kailan came up with a tale about how badly he needed the bonus from this job. About how he had to pay rent.

"My landlord is actually threatening to throw all my stuff out if I don't pay him soon, please! I need it this time, sir. I promise, when I am able to, I will donate triple the amount!"

Kailan was a very good actor. He even made sure to put a little bit of tremble in his voice, as though he were on the verge of tears. It was something that he had actually been practicing lately, knowing that such a feat might be needed.

In truth, he lived in an apartment that was in his own name, an apartment he had bought from the owner. His bank account had six figures, and it wasn't going to go down anytime soon. No one was going to touch it, no one. There was nothing in the world that Kailan was unwilling to say if it meant keeping the money in his own pocket, and not in the hands of someone else.

His boss, as usual, listened to his story and gave him the money he needed. Of course, some people didn't agree.

"He's just a greedy asshole," a woman whispered to her friend during lunch. "Did you know that he asked for a dowry from his ex-in-laws behind his ex-wife's back, and then when he broke it off with her, he refused to return it?"

The gossiping was a common occurrence. There were actually quite a few people in the office who did not like Kailan. They didn't realize that doing so only made it easier for him to convince his boss that he was being treated unfairly.

Kailan simply ignored them, choosing to turn his back to them and focus on getting his own meal heated up. It had only cost him a dollar, and while it tasted pretty bland, it was filling enough to have been worth just pennies. Even on things like food, Kailan hated spending much money.

After all, the more money he spent, the less money that he would end up having in the bank.

Inwardly, Kailan scoffed. Those dumbasses had easily bowed to his wishes. Why on Earth would he give away a chance to get money? He needed it; they didn't. It was as simple as that. They could be poor if they wanted to.

People like his co-workers just didn't understand how things really worked. They were soft and gentle, like that little bitch Clarissa was. Just the thought of her was enough to make Kailan's stomach curdle. He couldn't imagine ever being like her. It made him sick. No. He would never be like that! He was smarter than that; he was stronger than that!

And he was not going to return even a single penny. No matter how many notices they sent him, he would still be the richer one, still be the one with the most money. He would be the one who could see the world for what it really is. He just needed to be smart. He needed to stay on his feet.

It's just like the issue with his boss trying to steal his money for charity. That sort of thing; it's a trap that most people fall into. They get pulled into that game, where they're made to feel bad about taking care of themselves. The whole world was out to guilt trip him into giving up the money he'd worked so hard for. That's how Kailan saw it, at least.

He knew that it was something most people couldn't avoid. They were constantly being toyed with, having games played with them. They were always being suckered into helping other people at the cost of themselves. And Kailan knew that some of those people needed help. He knew it! But they could get it elsewhere. Why did it have to be him who had to help them? Why did he have to make that sacrifice?

He shouldn't!

He wouldn't!

Kailan refused to take part in that charity function, and he refused to let the thoughts of his co-workers get to him. This was something that he had to do. It was important. He had to stow away his pay checks for himself.

But it wasn't enough. Even if he had millions in his bank account. Even if he could easily retire and not need to work a single day for the rest of his life, he needed more. There was always that risk, lingering at the back of his mind. That possibility that things might not work out the way that they should. The chance that he might end up losing it all. It was haunting. It was an all-consuming concern. Something that Kailan refused to let happen.

That was why he had taken the pill. So that his greed for money could be satiated, and that his greed for always getting whatever monetary credits could be satiated.

He took it on a rainy Tuesday afternoon, and he dreamt — or at least, he thought it was a dream — that a dark and monstrous creature with sharp fangs and thorny skin had stood on top of him. The creature had dripped something onto him, thick drops of black, and the black had stained Kailan's clothing when he woke up the next day.

He was hungry, but food couldn't quite quench the yawning pit in his stomach. He used foundation to cover the black spots on his cheeks from where he had been dripped on, and then spent the day trying to figure out if his wish had come true or not; surely, if it had, then getting money would satisfy the ever-growing pit inside of his stomach.

It didn't take long for Kailan to realize what the pill had changed.

The pill had given him the skill to hack into any bank account. Any at all, even the most top-secret ones. It was as though there was another hand guiding his own, letting his fingers fly across the keys of the computer. The click clacks of keyboard keys being jammed down suddenly filled the air, flooding into it. It was as though the sound matched up with his heartbeat, or maybe as though his heartbeat matched up with the sound. Either way, it was a soothing thing.

He liked watching the code fill the screen, the boxes slide about. His hands moved as though they belonged to someone else, easily pulling up the information that he needed.

His neighbor had once gotten a bonus of a hundred grand because of his hard work. Kailan didn't allow that. It needed to be in better hands: his own. And the magic of the pill allowed that to happen. In just a few clicks — with just a few minutes of effort — the money was transferred into an off-shore bank account that belonged to Kailan, under a false name. He had created it specifically for this, letting his hands guide him through the motion.

And oh, it was worth it!

Now, there was a full hundred grand sitting in his account, right there within typing distance. He knew that it should be enough to give him a financial security that had never before been accessible. It should have been enough... but it wasn't.

Kailan knew that he would need to try and do it again.

He didn't care that the police suspected him instantly when he told them his reasoning for the pill. It was his money. His money. He should get all of it because he needed it.

That thought became an all-consuming burden. It pressed down against him, thundering loud and clear inside his skull. It made his chest ache, his stomach twist, and his hands shake. If he went more than a day without adding money to his balance, it was as though a great sickness came over him. All that he could think about was the fact that it would be so easy to make himself secure for the rest of his life. That all he would need to do was turn on the computer.

It felt, at times, like there was someone whispering that into his ear, bidding him to type faster, to make another transfer. At night, he dreamt that the demonic creature would sit over him in bed, drip onto him, and whisper.

The words felt almost real. The drops of black liquid burned on impact. Kailan stopped noticing it, and he stopped using concealer to cover it. The black stained his face like tear drops, one for each crime that he had committed thus far.

Getting more money became an obsession like it never had been before. And hacking into a bank, stealing everything, and adding it into his own account was so easy with the pill.

Kailan didn't even have to try and hide it! It was like someone else came along and did that for him! Truly, the pill was making all of his wildest dreams come true. Kailan didn't see any reason how this could come back and haunt him.

He didn't even see the fact that his skin was darkening every single day, to the point where it had gone completely black with no skin remaining, just darkness. Even if he wanted to put the concealer on, there was no way it would cover everything. Kailan would have to bathe in it — and even then, the black shade that his skin had taken on would simply come back.

And everywhere he walked, the world cried along. People would run away from him, not even look at him, and only those who had skin like him, gray, sickly skin, would tilt their heads at him.

He didn't care. He still had a mission he needed to complete. The world warped around Kailan. The whispering in the back of his head grew louder with each step that he took, with each transfer that he made. The pit inside of his chest grew wider until it felt like he was passing through a great canyon, and in that canyon, there was nothing but night.

Kailan was so focused on gaining more wealth, the world itself became nothing but background noise. It was nothing but static, existing on a seemingly separate dimension as Kailan. Just as the blackness of Kailan's skin seemed to darken the world around him, the single-minded focus that he had for gaining more wealth seemed to drown out everything else around him, until the only thing that still existed was his laptop, the bank, and the steadily rising numbers spread out over all of his many, many hidden accounts.

Unbeknownst to him, his previous actions had attracted something else other than the darkness. Wrath. Vengeance. Anger. Fury.

This should not have been surprising. As was clear to anyone who met him, Kailan was not a kind person. Even before he had taken the pill, Kailan had stolen from many people. He had taken money that wasn't his, he had taken food that wasn't his, and he had pushed others in front of buses so he could take promotions that weren't his.

The single-minded focus that Kailan had always maintained for gaining money had left him with very few friends, and very few people who gave half a damn about him.

It had also left Kailan as the victim of one person's fury, in particular.

That would be the fury of his ex-wife, who was so easily played that even she couldn't believe it. The fury of a woman that was scorned to the point where everyone ran away from her. Clarissa was furious toward Kailan.

They had been happy once, or so Clarissa thought. She had fallen in love with the false façade of a man who was seemingly down on his luck but was working hard at getting better. It was a front, of course, but not something that Clarissa would be able to see through for a very long time. After all, Kailan was an expert at acting. He had spent years perfecting his craft so that no one could look at him and see the truly devious, conniving, and greedy person he really was.

Clarissa believed the façade that she had been shown. She had fallen in love with Kailan, and then had that love and trust betrayed.

That jerk… that little jerk had demanded a dowry from her parents. He had demanded that they give him money, or he would dump her and break her heart, and she would never recover from it. And Clarissa's parents, who loved her so dearly, had agreed. They didn't want to be the reason that Clarissa was left alone, and so, they gave Kailan the dowry.

They had done it in secret, not wanting it to affect the marriage. They believed it would be used to make sure that Clarissa had a good life, that it would go to their honeymoon or as the down payment on a new house, that it would be used to treat Clarissa right.

None of those things happened. The money went into a hidden bank account instead, and Clarissa never saw a single penny of it. She didn't even know that it existed! The first few months were good, though, it wasn't because Kailan loved her. Clarissa would later find out that Kailan had been draining her bank account and putting the money into his own, that he was stealing her jewelry, pawning it, and then pocketing the cash.

There was no love between them, at least not on Kailan's end. He had just been using her to try and pad his checking account a little bit more. His threats to leave hadn't been cancelled, either. They were simply put on hold until he had milked Clarissa of every last cent that she had.

But eventually, he did just that. Eventually, he left her for the wolves, stealing every single penny in her account and running away. Well… sucks to be him. She filed a complaint to the police, and with the biggest, dirtiest scowl and snarl on his face, he had to return everything he had stolen from her. With interest. The dowry, though, had to go through the court. But the court was slow.

It seemed to take forever. There were bigger things going on in the world. The introduction of a strange new medication had flooded the court system with a series of lawsuits that had no precedent. Were these actions still illegal when a pill had allowed them to come into fruition? It was baffling and had caused all non-essential cases to be put on hold.

That meant that because the dowry wasn't a murder, and it didn't have any life-threatening consequences, the court system had deemed that it wasn't important enough to deal with just then. The very thought of it was enough to make her sick. There was something so disgustingly wrong with the idea of letting Kailan keep that money. It made Clarissa's blood boil in her veins. It made her heart brew with a rage that was like nothing else.

She wouldn't wait for the court to come to a decision. She would not. That man, that creature, had given her the horror of being left behind like trash. And she would turn him into trash.

That was the realization that Clarissa had come to. And it was also how she came up with a solution. The courts had paused all cases that were not considered to be completely essential. They didn't think that there was a way to prosecute anyone who had done a crime through the pill, for the pill technically circumvented it from being their own action.

Those few facts drifted about in Clarissa's mind for almost a week before she came to her decision. She would get her vengeance on Kailan and the courts all at the same time.

That was why she had taken the pill. Her desire?

To destroy, mutilate, annihilate, and then kill Kailan. She wanted to kill him. She wanted to wring his neck and watch him choke on the very air that he had taken from her. She wanted him to suffer agonizing pain for the heartache he had caused her and her family.

Was it cruel? Perhaps. But wasn't what Kailan did to her cruel as well? Didn't she deserve to enact her vengeance on the man who had left her with nothing, who had left her family with nothing?

Kailan had broken her heart, and she was determined to make him feel the same overwhelming pain and misery that she had gone through.

A single victory wasn't enough. She wanted, needed, him to suffer.

Some might think that this could have been accomplished even without the pill, that she could have simply killed him. But Kailan was smart. He was smart, and she had taken the pill to outsmart him and come up with a plan. Not only would it help her come up with a good way to stay out of prison for the crime, but it would help her get past the fact that Kailan really *was* a very intelligent person.

If Clarissa wanted to bring that filthy swine to his knees, she was going to have to play the same game as him. She was going to need to be smart and make sure that things went in her favor.

The moron was so greedy, he would walk out and scout out those he had to swindle. She didn't know why he did it, but she knew his schedule because of it, and she knew how to plan accordingly to take him down.

The pill gave her the idea and the courage for it. It left her with visions of a black, demonic thing and with whispers in her skull, but that was something that she would have no problem dealing with if it meant that this man was brought to his knees.

It hit her harder than it did most people, due to the nature of her wish. Clarissa was knocked out for two days and viciously ill for the third. The haunting visions of the creature never vanished. It seemed to be feeding off of the darkness that was naturally in her heart, making her chest ache and her hands tremble.

But it also filled her with even more determination than before, so she was looking forward to letting it take over her. She wanted Kailan to suffer.

When he was crossing the road, she would slam into him and run him over. That's the idea that she came up with. The perfect way to kill him so that he felt the same pain she had felt. She hoped that it broke all of his bones. She hoped that he didn't die instantly, that he had to deal with the agony of it.

A hacker friend of hers had already prepared an electronic will and a DNR form, as well as nominated her as a nominee for his insurance. He would not only suffer in real life as he dies under her car, but in the afterlife as he realizes the one fool he thought he had swindled a major victory off of was now using his money to do whatever she wanted.

Just the thought of it was enough to make Clarissa's mouth water. She was hungry for it — for his death, for that money, to finally get what she should never have lost in the first place. It was so close. It was within her reach!

It was a failproof plan. Unfortunately, she did not take Kailan's greed into account.

She should have.

Clarissa should have known that there would be a snag. That his own greed would have been enough to face down her wrath, to counter it. His greed was a beast, eternal and unending. It was something that few people could ever hope to stand up against.

She should have known it would have affected her plan.

The world should have known what would happen when two people who had taken the pill tried to battle each other.

Kailan was walking down the road, strutting arrogantly. He had robbed another bank just twenty minutes ago, and everyone was in a terror. But they had no reason to. It was money, and it had his name on it. Personally, Kailan was in a great mood. He had just added an obscene amount of money to his repertoire. He was thousands of dollars richer, and it had taken him practically no effort at all!

The pill was truly making his dreams become reality. With each penny that went into his pocket, he found himself a little bit more secure in the fact that he was never going to have to suffer the torment of being poor. He would never need to worry where his next meal was coming from or if he was going to be able to pay his bills.

Kailan would be set for his entire life, no matter what happened. And he would just keep on padding those accounts and creating more of a buffer.

He knew he was being greedy, something inside of him was screaming that at him, but he didn't care. Kailan knew that he was forcing more and more people down the same path that he himself was so violently trying to avoid. He was forcing them to struggle with suddenly empty accounts and with bills that they didn't know how they would be able to pay.

It should have made him feel guilty. It should have made him feel *something*. But it didn't. At least, nothing bad. It just made Kailan feel more content with himself and with his own future. More content that things were finally starting to go exactly the way that they were supposed to.

As long as he could get the money, he would have it. That was the simple fact of the world, as Kailan saw it. He deserved that money. The pill would let him have that money. The whispering in the back of his mind, it agreed with him. It told Kailan that the money was meant to be rightfully his, that he was meant to have something no one else ever could.

He was supposed to be rich. The richest man in the world!

And then he saw the ATM. Something just snapped as he saw a man withdraw cash from it. It was like that pit inside of him finally finished splitting, severing Kailan from his sanity and his concept of what was right and what was wrong. Something ugly spilled into him, that blackness finally taking hold of his mind and forcing him forward, so that he was propelling himself out of his usual path and toward the man at the ATM.

Rage filled him, threatening to drown out everything else.

"Go," said the creature, right in Kailan's ear. "Go! Don't let him take your money. Don't let him! Make him stop. That's your money, and he shouldn't have it!"

The creature was right. How dare he? How dare he use his money? He wouldn't have it! He wouldn't let him!

"No! Go away!"

He ran toward the ATM. A buzzing filled Kailan's mind. It was like someone had shoved an angry hornet's nest inside of his skull. The whispering mixed with the buzzing until it managed to blank out Kailan's mind. The sound was inside of his very bones. It was inside of his teeth.

It was all consuming.

The man who was withdrawing the money looked at him strangely, putting the money in his wallet and backing away. "Back off, buddy. Don't be weird."

"It is mine! Mine! Give it to me! It's MINE!" Kailan charged at him, slamming him onto the sidewalk.

"Piss off, dude!" The man glared.

Kailan tried to punch him. His swing missed; he wasn't the most athletic person, and the pill had done nothing to change that. His swings were wild and frothy, and none of them landed.

The man, on the other hand, was built like a brick wall. He punched him back, slapped him, and then kneed him in the stomach. "Jeez, arrogant much? Just piss off."

It sent bolts of pain through Kailan. Wheezing, he doubled over, staggering as he clutched at his gut. The buzzing was still so loud that he couldn't think through it. He didn't fully comprehend what had just happened. It was like a part of him was gone; a part of Kailan had just completely shut off, leaving him with no rational thought.

Without even looking back, the man walked away. Kailan wanted to scream. The man was walking off with his money! His! But then he looked at the ATM, and he realized: why did he have to take a poor beggar's money when he had the bank in front of him?

With a heavy snarl, he started beating the ATM. He cracked the screen and pressed buttons upon buttons. He wanted it. He wanted the green cash that was inside of it! He didn't care if his knuckles were bleeding; he needed all the money. All of it. It was his! All his! No one else! His and his alone! His eyes spotted a crowbar to the side. Or he thought it was a crowbar, and he took it and used it to smash the machine. Why. Wouldn't. The. Money. Come. OUT?

The buzzing in his brain got louder and louder. It was an obsession. It was more than that. It was the only reason that his heart was still beating. The reflection of the demonic creature was visible on the cracked screen of the ATM. While the face was hidden beneath its black hood, there was still no denying the fact that the twisted thing seemed to be radiating a sort of happiness, as though it was pleased with how far Kailan had fallen.

"STOP, POLICE!"

He heard sirens behind him and shouting, but he didn't care. He used all of his strength and cracked the glass, and the metallic crowbar hit a wire in the machine. Hundreds of volts coursed through his body, and the last thought he had before everything dissolved into a world of pain and coldness was, *No... I need more money! NOW!*

And just like that, Kailan was dead. Fried via electrical current to an extent no human being had been fried before. He didn't know what his death had started.

The police were left shocked, reeling with the sight before them. It was only a matter of moments before the news crew hit the scene of the crime and began doing a report on the entire thing.

"It was like nothing I've ever seen before," said Officer Ryan. "I don't know what the hell was wrong with him, but... well, you can't see it now on account of all that charring, but there was something wrong with his skin, even before he got zapped. I wonder... shit, I shouldn't say this."

"We'll keep it off the record," promised the reporter. "What do you wonder?"

Officer Ryan scratched the back of his neck and then admitted, "I wonder if it had something to do with that pill circulating around. You know, they say it can mess with your skin. I haven't taken it so I don't know a whole lot about it, but… it just makes me wonder."

It made the reporter wonder, too. This was far from the first strange death that she had reported on in the last several months. After the announcement of the so-called miracle pill, it seemed like the whole world was teetering on the edge of an abyss. She just didn't know what to think about it… but she did as she promised, and she kept Officer Ryan's thoughts off record during her report.

Exactly two blocks over, a whistling Clarissa was driving down the road when it came in the news.

"… and we have a new report down here in Grace Frost. A madman locals identified as Kailan was fried to his death via electricity when he slammed a crowbar into an ATM screaming, he needed more money, all the money in the world. We can only wonder…"

Clarissa didn't care what else the reporter said. It was like something in her head had completely blanked out. Or maybe that wasn't accurate. It was like a part of her brain had just gone into overdrive. The thought of this report being true, it messed with what had become a fundamental part of Clarissa's very existence.

Since taking the pill, her entire life had revolved around the plan she was supposed to carry out today, and now, they were telling her that Kailan was already dead? That was impossible. He was *her* target. Hers to kill and conquer! Hers to murder! Hers! Hers! Hers! HERS! No one was allowed to kill him! NO ONE!

The pit inside of her was desperate to be filled, and the only thing that could fill it was having Kailan dead and gone… by her own hands! To think that he had managed to off himself, that he had died at someone else's hands, it was too much.

She wouldn't stand it. She wouldn't stand it! She wouldn't stand anyone or anything killing Kailan, even if it was himself!

"You've lost your purpose," said the creature, sitting in the passenger seat. "I will give you a new one. His body is dead, but his soul still exists. Find another way to kill him. You must do this. He's meant to die by your hands."

The creature was right.

Clarissa was meant to kill Kailan, and no one else. That was what was supposed to happen! And she knew that this was a fate she would need to solve now. A problem that she couldn't put off. Unlike the dowry, still held up in the court system where it would probably stay forever, this was something that couldn't just be left to sit around. She had to change it.

Clarissa had taken the pill so that she could kill Kailan and get away with it.

She wouldn't let anything take that from her.

With a loud roar and a slam of the accelerator, she drove right into the side of the bridge, over the river, and straight down into it. There was a bang as her head impacted against the windscreen at the harsh jerk, and a splash as her car went deeper and deeper into the river.

The glass shattered. Blood poured from her face, and water rushed into the car, filling it up with a strange hiss. The creature vanished from its spot on the seat beside her, and Clarissa's vision swam. The concussion was severe, but even worse, was the fact that the car was filling up with water. It was only a matter of moments before the inside of the car was entirely flooded.

Water rushed into her lungs. The salt of the ocean stung her eyes and throat, and made her choke. It pushed all the air from her — but she didn't struggle. Clarissa didn't even try to unhook her seat belt. No, this was exactly what she wanted. It was exactly what needed to happen.

If I can't kill Kailan in real life… then I'll kill him in the afterlife! The madwoman thought one last time before she, too, succumbed to the cold darkness.

Over on the bridge, someone shook their head, absolutely tired of these fools who wished for nothing but single missions. Why kill yourself when you had all the pride needed in the world? After all, the pill could fix anything these days. All you needed to do was pop it down once, and all of your strife would vanish — just like that.

In the distance, police sirens filled the air. The man clucked his tongue once more and then continued on his way.

The world spun on, even without Kailan and Clarissa in it.

Chapter Nine

ASTER AND PRIDE HAD ALWAYS gone together. Ever since he was young, he had a problem with pride. He thought that he was good, that he was even the best. As a child, Aster had very few friends, largely because he refused to play any games that he wasn't good at, and he was very boastful whenever he won. A bit of a sore winner.

It was a bit of an obsession. Aster wanted to be the best at everything he did. He took great pride in his appearance. He took great pride in his grades and the state of his homework. He took great pride in the way that he spoke, adopting a refined manner of speech that grated on everyone's nerves.

And as he grew older, the strong sense of pride that he had for himself continued to grow and grow. Soon, it was his home life that he took pride in, the car that he drove, the brand of clothes that he wore, the state of his house. When he got a job, he was obsessed with always becoming Employee of the Month, and when he joined the Police Academy, he was obsessed with getting the top grades in the class and getting the best marks at the gun range.

If Aster was going to do something, then he was going to be the best at it. That was just the simple way that he dealt with things. There was no point in doing something that he was a failure at, no matter how much fun it was. Aster never did anything that wasn't a boon to how he looked, or to his own sense of self-esteem.

He had more pride in his thin, wiry frame than anyone in the world should ever be able to obtain.

Sometimes, this was a good thing. Sometimes, it was a bad thing. No matter how it was viewed, it was simply how Aster was. Everyone knew it, everyone, even his parents. But no matter how much they tried to remove it out of him, it just didn't work. Because for Aster, pride was everything.

No lessons or lectures or helpful bits of advice had ever been able to change how he viewed the world. And it never would be.

There is nothing above pride. Nothing. If one doesn't have pride, then they don't have anything. Aster thought, shaking his head as he finished his patrol.

It was his eighteenth patrol of the day, and he had collected eight fines. Eight. Because the idiots on the streets simply refused to follow the rules. Had they done so and been like him, prideful and proper, then they wouldn't have to be fined like that. And insulted like that.

They always acted as though Aster was the bad guy for calling them out on things! They seemed to think that they were above the law, and for no reason. But what made them so special? Being a slob and not following the rules, that wasn't something to be proud of!

It always made Aster feel more vindicated to think that he had knocked someone down a peg or two. *Ha! The look on their faces were worth it. I don't get it. They all know what the laws in this city are. If they just followed them, I wouldn't have to hand out so many fines. It's absolutely ridiculous. And then for them to act like I'm the bad guy? I'm the only one following the rules! It's like I'm the only one in this city who's got any pride for themselves.*

It was a thought that Aster often had. He didn't understand why people tried to behave like they were above the law. They were just so… lackluster about things. It wasn't just the law, either. Aster found himself in the middle of a city that just didn't care about their personal appearance, that just didn't care about how they looked or acted or what other people thought of them.

It was like no one here had any self-respect or appreciation for the fact that they could do better if they only put in a little bit of effort.

Well, didn't matter.

Aster had enough pride to make up for everyone.

As he walked inside the police station, he spotted his boss, Officer Ryan Shield, glaring at him as he stomped to his location. Aster sighed, rolling his eyes as he stood to attention. Why was he meant to bow down to and salute this person? Why? His pride was clearly better than his! He was the only one with the right attitude in this building; he deserved that position! He deserved everyone's respect!

Meanwhile, Officer Ryan was a little on the hefty side, with a scraggly beard and hair that always seemed windswept. Right now, there was powdered sugar on his fingers and a coffee stain on his tie. How did he get the title of chief when he wasn't even able to take pride in how he looked? He was the head of the entire office, for God's sake! And here he was, looking like someone who had just rolled into their first day at the Academy.

Aster always kept his uniform in top shape. He never let it get stained or dirty. Every night after work, he washed, ironed, and starched his shirt. His ties always matched his socks. His face was always clean-shaven, and his hair always done up. He took a great amount of pride in his appearance.

"You…," the man growled. "What did you do, you arrogant, prideful idiot?"

His boss was angry. Very angry. But Aster didn't care. He wasn't going to bow to the man. He wasn't going to bow to the man in front of him. Because if he did, then he would be breaking his pride, and it would hurt him a lot more than anything else.

"I did nothing wrong," Aster said insistently. "I simply made sure they understood their place against me, and nothing else."

"I don't care what you think of yourself and what everyone else thinks of you, you idiot! Your job is to be a public servant, a man who serves and protects! And punching someone in the face when they threw law your way, and telling them they had to pay a fine because you said so, are not the right things to do!" Officer Ryan growled. "So, this is what you will do. You will apologize. Write a written apology, and deliver it by hand to the people you punched! DO. YOU. UNDERSTAND?"

"No," Aster replied instantly. Because that would be below his pride to do so, and he refused to do anything that was below his pride. Anything. "I will not. I did the right thing. I know what is right and—"

The next thing he knew, he was being punched in the face so hard that he could still feel the pain. His head snapped backwards, a pain shooting down his neck and straight into his spine. Worse was the wetness that welled up under his nose as hot trails of blood dribbled down his face and over his lips in fat, red drops.

It got on his tie, leaving an awful stain.

Already, Aster could feel the way that the skin on the side of his face was starting to swell, no doubt a black eye in the making. More than the pain, Aster was struck by how this was going to make him look. It was a horrible realization, to know that he was going to have to walk around looking like some drunk who had gotten into a fist fight.

And his tie! How was he going to get the blood out of it? It was silk. Silk!

"Officer Aster Moore…," the Commander of his base snarled. "You are discharged, dishonorably, from all your duties for assaulting a member of the public, for disregarding the rules, and for refusing to follow the orders of your superior! In other words, you are fired."

A hush fell over the unit. No one liked Aster due to his prideful nature and his insistence that he was the absolute best at everything, but they were all interested in seeing how this was going to pan out. It was fascinating.

They thought that maybe there might be a fight. Aster loved his job, and they thought that maybe he would try to argue his way back into the unit. But no, that was something that Aster would refuse to stoop to.

He had been fired, and that was that. He was done.

At least, that was what the Commander of his base thought. He left the station with his head held high, but even he knew that the case that was being filed against him would break his pride completely. Not to mention the fact that everyone was going to be talking about him from now on. It was absolutely horrible. The realization that he was going to need to live this down — that people were going to be spreading rumors and gossiping about him — it made him feel ill.

And he couldn't have that. He. Could. Not. Have. That. His pride was much more important to him than anything else in this world. Anything.

The first thing that Aster did upon getting home was rush to the computer, where he ordered next-day delivery of the strongest concealer that he could find. He treated his tie, washed, ironed, and primmed his clothing for the next day, and then spent the night lying on the couch with an ice pack on his face to try and bring down the swelling.

The concealer arrived late the next day, and Aster made sure to stay home until then. He used the concealer to hide the bruising around both eyes and the discoloring on his nose. Then, content with how he looked much more put together, he took a deep breath and stepped outside for the day.

Aster instantly regretted it.

News traveled fast in their town, and it seemed as though everyone was already talking about him. When he went to his usual coffee shop — one that was preferred by officers who worked at the nearby station — he was met with nothing but people whispering about him.

Whispering. Ha! Were they even trying to be quiet? Aster could hear every word that they said, and it wasn't nice.

"Look," a blonde woman said and pointed as Aster waited in line for his coffee.

Her friend, a tall man with dark hair, answered, "It's him, isn't it?"

"The idiot officer." The blonde agreed.

The man asked, "Did you hear what he did?"

The woman shook her head. "It looks like he was fired! But I didn't hear what he did to get canned. I mean, I can take a couple of wild guesses.

"Look at him!" The man laughed. "He's an absolute lunatic, you know? I heard that he punched someone for parking in a fire lane. Got canned right there on the spot."

"Oh my god!" the blonde woman yelled slightly louder. She picked up her coffee when it was ready. "I can't even imagine doing something like that. You have to be a certain kind of crazy for..."

The words trailed off as they gathered their drinks and left. Aster snatched up his own coffee when it was ready, spinning around and scowling.

He snarled at everyone who was talking behind his back. How dare they? Couldn't they see that he did the right thing? He could never be wrong! He was always right! He knew the best, more so than anyone else in the world, and his pride refused to let him admit, that perhaps, he had messed up.

No, that would be going below his pride, and he refused to do that. He refused to do that. Refused. Refused. Refused.

To Aster, it was everyone else who had messed up. They had someone brilliant like him helping to protect them, and they just let him go. They fired him, just like that! It was an unreasonable offense. It was something that he simply couldn't abide by or allow to continue. He was going to need to make sure that they all realized they were in the wrong, that Officer Ryan had put the town in danger by letting go his star officer.

Him!

Aster was the only one keeping order in this town! He was the only one who cared enough to make sure that people abided by the rules. And when they didn't, well, he was the only one who cared enough to make sure that they were punished for it!

Aster honestly couldn't understand why no one else seemed to acknowledge that. Why were they all acting like this? Talking about him behind his back and siding with Officer Ryan... had Officer Ryan paid them off? Was that what happened? The man must have done something similar to that, or else people wouldn't be acting this way. They would understand that Aster was correct in how he had been handling the situation.

He would have to do something to show him. To show that former boss of his and the people in the city that he was always right. That there was no one else more right in this world, no one more deserving of respect in this world, than him. And he knew exactly what he had to get.

He had been listening to the news about a ground-breaking pill that was allowing people to get whatever they wanted, no matter how impossible it seemed. He had also heard how it was making people go mad, making people go insane and lose their minds. But that was not anything to worry about. Not for him. He wouldn't go mad because he was in control of himself. Him, and him alone. And no one else. And that pill would fall into his hands. And then he would show them all why he was right. The pill gave everyone the power to do whatever they wanted.

The other people, the ones who had gotten sick, it was because they were weak. They didn't have the self-control needed to handle an immense power like a wish-granting pill. They might have wanted to get rid of their strife, but they didn't actually deserve that gift, and because they didn't deserve it —

because they didn't use it correctly — they had suffered for it.

At least, that was Aster's view of things.

Meanwhile, he was so confident in himself that he believed he would be above the side effects that the pill created. He would be able to handle the powers trapped in that little powdery form even when no one else had managed it.

He would use it to make sure everyone knew that he would not do anything that seemed below his pride. No bowing down to others. No saluting others. No listening to others. Except him. Him, and him alone.

Because he deserved it.

The pill was difficult to obtain. It used to be that anyone with the cash for it could show up somewhere and make the purchase, but now, the government was crashing down hard on those who were still selling the pill, and it got difficult to do when half the government was profiting from it, and the other half had the signature gray skin of someone who had taken the pill.

Aster warred with himself temporarily. Getting an illegally-bought substance should have been beneath him, but knowing that the pill would help the world see the truth balanced it out. He ended up buying the pill, not from a pharmacy, government building, or police station, but from the daughter of a governor who was profiting from the pill.

They met in an upscale restaurant outside of town, where they had a lovely steak dinner and then exchanged the pill at the end of the night.

"Never call me again," she warned.

"I won't," said Aster, confident in the fact that he would never need to.

Then he went home. The pill itself was small and white, and it left powdery smears on his fingers. Curious, he cracked it in half… and found that the inside contained a sort of black glittery substance. Very strange! He'd never seen a pill like this before. Then again, he supposed that was because this was a magical pill.

He popped both halves into his mouth and licked all of the powder off his fingers.

He didn't care. The minute that he had taken the pill, he already knew things were changing. It burned and scraped his throat on the way down, and it hit his stomach like a barrel of bricks. Aster's legs crumpled beneath him, and he fell to the floor. It felt like the weight of the entire universe was pressing down on him. It made all of his muscles protest and his bones creak.

He was so taken off guard that he didn't realize it was because something very heavy was sitting on him. At least, not until a dark hand with thorny skin and sharp nails reached down and stroked too long fingers over the back of one of Aster's hands.

It left smears of a very deep dark black in its wake. Five lines that ran the length of the five fingers on Aster's hand, all the way down to his wrist.

The creature said something, but the voice was faint and scratchy, impossible to make out. Still, the words sunk into Aster, filling him with the sense of being praised. It made his head spin, and his heart thud about in his chest.

He tried to speak, to ask what was going on, but couldn't so much as croak out a single word. A sense of accomplishment filled him, funneling into the pit that had formed inside of him, spreading out and separating his heart from the rest of his body.

Aster didn't know if the weight vanished. All he knew was that when he woke up again, the creature was gone, and the black lines remained. But that didn't bother him. He could just find a pair of fine-looking black leather gloves to cover them up.

The next day, he got a call stating that the people who had charged him with assault were apologizing and had taken it back. They were sorry for pressing charges and for arguing; they admitted that Aster had been in the right the entire time.

He didn't care. What did people like that matter? They were so far beneath Aster that he had nearly forgotten about their existence in the first place!

It was late in the day before his phone rang again, and this time, it was a call that Aster was far, far more interested in. His former boss called him and said he was getting a promotion for doing the right thing. And that was what he wanted to hear. That he had his job back, that his boss knew Aster was the best officer who had ever worked in this damn police station, and that Officer Ryan had been in the wrong while Officer Aster had been right.

People accepting his pride was all needed. He didn't care who he hurt because of it. He didn't care what he hurt because of it, and he sure didn't care why he hurt so many because of it. The only thing that mattered was his pride. And his pride alone.

As a child, it had been one thing. Something that could be managed and worked around. As a young adult working at a gas station, it was manageable even if it did get on everyone's nerves. But there was danger to be found in a police officer who thought that his word was finite, who felt that there was no one else who could have a correct view of things.

Aster was walking a dangerous line, and it wasn't even something that he was aware of.

Two weeks later, he said to his boss when he was asked to go help out in cleaning the sewers, that he thought it wasn't the job for someone with as much pride as him. To think that Officer Ryan would think that a man of Aster's standard would ever stoop to such a filthy job! The sewers were quite literally filled with shit. They were not a place where Aster would ever go, no matter how much money was behind it.

He was the best officer in the city, and he deserved to be treated as such!

"No," said Aster, face twisting into a sneer that showed off his teeth. The flesh of his gums was starting to turn an ugly shade of gray, and the enamel of his molars seemed to be less white than they had been even just three days ago. "I'm much better than a dirty garbage man. Go and get someone else to do it."

Ryan agreed and found someone else while Aster casually strutted out, acting like he owned the entire town. That's how Aster felt these days. Thanks to the power of the pill, there was nothing that he couldn't do; there was nothing that he wasn't able to turn down. Aster was practically king of the world! It was a position that he felt he honestly deserved, and no one would ever be able to convince the man of anything else.

He would do whatever he wanted, put his legs on a bar stool, slump down on whatever couches he could find. His pride in being the best was overruling his pride in caring about what other people thought of him. Look at that! Aster could do whatever the hell he wanted and not be asked to stop. Because if he bowed to anyone, it would be below his pride. And it was paying off.

He was promoted, again and again, until he became Chief of Police in the district. Everyone clearly knew exactly who he was. Exactly what he deserved, and now, he had his own office, his. No one dared to look at him or stand up to him, because they knew he would never agree with them. Agreeing with someone else was below his pride. It was thoroughly below his pride, and he would never dare to break it.

Aster was at the top. He was above anyone else in this town, but it was more than that. He had begun to view himself as something more than just human. The whispering in the back of his head had planted the idea there, though Aster didn't realize it.

Where else would he have gotten the idea that the pill had made him into a god?

Well, maybe it *was* just the pill. Maybe it was a delusion. Whatever it was, it had started to affect Aster's view of things in an even greater manner. The cuticles of his nails were now midnight black. The whites of his eyes had become an abyss. He was a god stuck dealing with mortals who didn't understand that — and it was not a lack of understanding that could be allowed to last.

"Yes. I am the only thing that this world needs or deserves." He nodded to himself, looking at his city from his office. "But do they truly deserve me? They still continue to stand up to me, expecting me to bow. Tch, filthy mortals."

Things had to change. After all, there was still one thing standing in Aster's way.

There was still a government, and the government still gave him orders. He couldn't deny them; somehow, they were immune to everything he tried. Why didn't they see that Aster was a god? Why couldn't they understand that he was above their silly little governing system?

He had to bow to them, he knew it, but his pride wouldn't allow him. He was the only one who people should bow to, and not the other way around. Not again. Never again.

The fact that the government seemed to be unaffected by anything that Aster did was an all-consuming, maddening thought. It followed him everywhere, haunting him every moment of the day. Even when Aster didn't actually have to deal with the government, he was thinking about it. He was thinking about the fact that those idiots thought they knew better than him!

They didn't, of course. Not as far as Aster was concerned. And so, he decided that he was going to need to do something. He would make one final stand and convince the government to release full and total power over to Aster.

No. These mortals… these simpletons don't deserve me! Aster thought madly, getting up and pacing around in his office.

The whispering agreed with him. It told him that he was going down the right path, that he was meant to rule over everyone.

He remembered the incident that had happened. Aster couldn't stop thinking about it. It was like the memory was being played in his mind on a loop, a constant recording that would never end. With the other chiefs in the districts, he was attending a meeting with the governor when the governor called him out on his prideful attitude and asked him to tone it down. He refused to tone it down. That was what he said.

Everyone else had gone silent. The other chiefs had heard about Aster, and they knew that he was a touchy being, that the slightest provocation could set him off like a live wire being tripped. Everyone was interested in seeing how this would turn out.

Would the governor, Rick Mathies, fold like everyone else?

No!

To their surprise, Rick Mathies held his ground! In fact, he was furious that Aster would dare try and defy his order. He threatened to fire him, and had halved the funding to his department. Slashed it, just like that! As if he had the right to try and control anything that Aster was doing!

Bowing was below his pride, but Rick didn't care. Governor Mathies had forced him, him, the great Aster Moore, to bow down to him. How? How? Did he not stand higher than these mortals? These ingrates? Didn't he deserve to be the one to ask everyone to bow to him? Then why was there always someone, someone who would ask him to back off? Who would ask him to bow? That wasn't right! That wasn't right at all!

"You are above the mortals," said the creature, suddenly appearing beside the window. "You deserve to be with the gods, where they will see you for who you really are. A truly great man. Someone who deserves the ultimate form of respect. Go to them. Go to them!"

The words seemed to engulf Aster. He had been teetering on the edge of insanity for some time now, perhaps since even before he took the pill. The commentary by the creature was as overwhelming as Aster's need to be above everyone else. He stood up so fast that it knocked his chair over. He slammed a hand on the table.

Thinking about that meeting with the governor was too much. Aster was back in his own home at the moment, but the walls seemed too small. His eyes landed on a butcher knife on the counter, but he knew that was beneath him. He didn't want people to view this as a suicide. He wanted it to be seen as the sacrifice that it truly was; an exchange of a mortal body for one that would never again know strife. He rushed over to the window and opened it.

"No! I will not bow! Not anymore! Everyone is below me! Everyone is beneath me!" Aster bellowed; head shoved out the window. It caught the attention of the people milling about below, who turned their gazes to the open window to see what all the fuss was about. "I am joining the gods! I will always be on top of everyone! No one will ask me to bow ever again!"

With a mad shout and a lunge, the Chief of the District Police, Aster Moore, jumped out of his window. For a moment, he was in the air, soaring through it. Wind wrapped around his body, pressing into him. It felt like he was flying.

He screamed like a madman and laughed as he fell. But Aster felt no fear. He could only see this as one final victory; he was finally releasing himself from the mortal confines of this human form, putting aside all the slobs and the sloths who inhabited this planet of existence so that he could ascend to the next; a higher form of being where Aster could be lauded as the god that he truly was.

Everyone could only watch as the screaming, cackling body fell to the ground, and then there was absolute silence. Silence and horror. A mother screamed and covered the eyes of her child, but it was no use. Everyone on the street had seen what happened. A completely dark body, smashing to the ground and corrupting the ground itself.

The blackness seemed to spread through his blood, spilling out onto the pavement. It seeped through the cracks in the cement and into the ground beneath it, where the soil devoured the blackness like poison. The very air around the body appeared to have been altered as it shimmered like it was trapped in a heat wave, dulling and dimming the longer that the remains sat there.

Aster had managed to sour the very Earth upon which he died, just like he had soured the lives of everyone who he had come into contact with over the years.

"Oh god, he finally snapped!" a policeman exclaimed. "That prideful idiot... He... what on Earth happened to his brain, and how did someone appoint *him* to be the District Head of the police?"

No one had an answer.

A hush fell over the city as the police set up a crime scene. Even as they did, people looked on at the man's remains. The darkened skin. The way he had lost his glow. His madness, and they knew exactly what could have caused this.

By now, rumors had spread about what the pill could make a person do, spilling into the world, into existence, and the government had to crack down on how many of the pills were actually still out there. And still, people had wondered if it was true. After all, conspiracy theories were a dime a dozen! There were still people who thought the moon landing was faked. Hell, there were still people who thought that the moon was made out of cheese!

But this was something different. At least, to those who had watched Officer Aster Moore's slow descent into madness, and who had now been there to witness the end to his life, they had been given irrefutable proof as to what the pill was capable of causing.

The only thing that went through their heads was, *oh god, the pill causes people to go mad and kill themselves!*

The pill that seeped darkness into the minds of innocent human beings.

The pill had been created to eradicate strife, but instead, it had produced an entirely new problem. It was something that the media kept trying to report on, but the governing powers that had helped develop the pill were trying to keep the truth of the matter under wraps. They didn't want to admit that they had released a substance so foul and deadly into the world.

It would have been one thing if the pill had just caused an adverse mental reaction. Plenty of medications had side effects like that. The problem was that there didn't appear to be an explanation for the way that it brought an ugly, terrible darkness into those who took it. There seemed to be no way to explain the fact that it had a unique ability to ruin the very air that surrounded a person who took it. But one thing was clear, selfishness and greed had created the demise of the people.

The news tried to cover this foul darkness and how badly it was affecting the world around them, but as instantly as it appeared in the news, it died. The general public didn't care as long as their dreams were coming true. After all, only they mattered, no one else.

And the government, well, they had been supporting this from the start. They would never admit to having messed up so badly. They would never admit that they had caused the inadvertent downfall of the human race.

If they knew what the darkness was, they wouldn't admit to that, either.

And as usual, people decided to just ignore these fallacies and continue on as if there was nothing wrong with the pill.

One man, though, looked at the dead body, rooted to his spot. He coughed lightly and walked away, his eyes holding a glint never seen before. A thought had just appeared in the back of the man's mind, and it was rapidly consuming him.

Fear. Fear of what had happened to the man happening to him. Fear of death. The same death he had been dreading since he found out about his condition. No, it would not take him away as well. It would not.

He would make sure of it.

Chapter Ten

SLATER WAS NEVER A SIMPLE MAN. Never. He had always been different from everyone else, mainly because he had come from a rich family. A family of people who had always been the epitome of business and commerce, who had roots so deep it got hard to figure out how deep they went.

His family was, simply put, loaded. As such, Slater had grown up knowing all of the luxuries that the world had to offer. He had grown up knowing caviar, wild salmon, and the richest, sweetest chocolates that the world had to offer. He had never known what it was like to be poor, or to go hungry, or to wear shoes that didn't fit quite right.

Of course, there were other people like that. Slater was rich, but that didn't make him completely unique.

In fact, that was not the reason why he wasn't normal.

His lack of normalcy went much deeper than that. It was something in his brain. A misfire, maybe, or perhaps simply a firing that everyone else was lacking. You see, Slater was a very curious person, and he was always trying to figure out how things worked.

Since the first day he could speak, he would ask questions. There was no end to his need for knowledge, and nothing that he didn't want to know more about. It wasn't as though Slater had a particular hobby that he was obsessed with. It's not as though he only wanted to learn everything that the world had to offer about a single specific thing, like cars or trains or the weather.

Rather, Slater simply was hungry for learning. The more information that he was able to absorb, the happier of a person he became. As such, Slater was constantly trying to figure out how different things worked.

He would question everyone and everything. His parents. His friends. His teachers. His grandparents and later on, even computers and the Internet. If there was a topic out there, Slater wanted to learn more about it.

Why were planes able to fly? Why had they never been able to figure out how many stars were in the universe? Why did bodies need air to function? Why did plants grow in the shapes and heights that they did? He wanted to know about machines and the Earth. He wanted to know about science and history.

And, perhaps more importantly, Slater wanted to know about death.

In fact, he wanted to know about death and the afterlife more than anything else in the world. It was his favorite thing to ask people about — but he never got the same answer. Everyone had a different take on what would happen after death. They all had their own unique thoughts on the matter, their own individual beliefs.

As such, Slater was never able to find something that could give him a concrete answer to his question. At least, not for many, many years. It was well into his fifties that he finally got a proper answer, in an article that he read.

People, no matter how far they have gone, have categorized two constants, two states of being for their existence. Life and Death.

Life, which personified what people did when they were conscious, when they were able to control and properly understand whatever they were doing and whatever it was possible for them to do. It was something that they did when they were alive, when they were actually worth something. It was strange, what Life and Death was. It was strange, what Life and Death personified. It was strange, when we ask the question, "What is Death?"

The answer to that is simple. **Life is a beautiful lie, and Death is a dreadful truth.**

You may have heard the proverb before because it's exactly what it says. When people are alive, they can do whatever they want, lie to themselves that they would be alive forever. That nothing would stop them from doing what they wanted. But that was not the case. That was simply not the case at all. For each breath they took in and let out, for each birthday they celebrated, they came closer and closer to the truth that was Death.

Life is ultimate, but Death is absolute. No one can escape Death, destruction, or oblivion because Death was the end to all things. Just like no one can escape Life, as it is the start of all things. But it was impossible to think, or even believe, that anyone could remain alive forever. Everyone will all eventually end.

It was a strange concept, to go to sleep and never wake up again. To dive into something that you simply cannot know or remember ever thinking about. No one knows what happens once they die, what happens to a being, a creature, when they finally take the plunge into complete darkness. No one knows what happens to them when Death finally claims them. But everyone knows one thing, and one thing only.

Death is always waiting, in the end, for everyone and everything. No matter how much someone tries to run away from it; no matter how much someone tries to fight it. No matter how much someone tries to not think about it, it is always there. Always waiting.

And because of that, Slater decided death was something to be afraid of.

In fact, it might have been the only thing in the world that was worth being genuinely terrified of. It was not like sharks or thunder; there were no concrete evidence of what would happen after someone's heart beats for the final time, or what would await the soul and the spirit once the flesh and body were finally shoved deep into the sheltered ground.

It was concept that no one understood, that no one had proof of, that no one even knew about. Oh, people had tried over the years! But look at how many religions had started up. Look at how many people claimed that their belief was the only true belief — only for an opposing and very different rite to claim the same thing.

Truly, it was something that people couldn't ever hope to understand. Death was finite. It was the one thing that simply stopped, that had no answer. People understood how it worked on a physical body. There were countless books on how internal organs functioned, how certain things were needed to make sure that the flesh of the body stayed healthy.

People had done lectures on blood flow and oxygen; they had done dissertations on what could bring an end to a human's existence. But they didn't know what happened after that.

One could not just come back from the dead. If someone died, then they would be gone. Just… a memory, and nothing else. Not able to influence anyone or anything, not able to see where the future took them. Not able to see how the world changed and moved. Not able to see anything. Anything except for darkness. For that was death.

Darkness.

And darkness terrified Slater. It hadn't when he was younger, but the more that Slater learned about the world, the more he became afraid of losing it. What would happen to him when his body ceased to function? He wasn't getting any younger! Slater was no fool. He knew that he didn't have much life left ahead of him; he knew that people rarely lived to be a hundred these days, especially not with how the current state of the world was.

Slater would eventually have to meet his maker, and it would probably be soon. Just the thought of it was enough to make Slater's hands shake. He would reach for another cigarette, struggling to get the lighter on, and then letting the deep drag of the nicotine help ease his frayed nerves.

He didn't want to slumber in eternal darkness. He didn't want to die. He refused to go down without any idea of what awaited him, without any idea of what was going to happen to him. Without even knowing what was going to happen to his family.

Family was very important to Slater. The thought of one day losing them — losing track of them — it was a unique sort of dread. Slater would liken it to getting drunk one night and then waking up naked in a tiger's pen. The kind of dread that snuck up on him but still managed to make sense.

Slater loved his family. The thought of being away from them was an unwelcoming one.

His family had always been his biggest joy, and he wanted to see where their future took them. He wanted to see how his grandchildren would grow up. He wanted to see how his children would go through the same problems he had to face, and how they would handle them. Slater wanted to know that they would be safe, and he wanted to know that they would do great things.

Once his body died, that was it. There was no proof that his consciousness would linger. There was no proof that he would be able to stay in the realm as an unseen force and watch over them. Slater needed to see what became of his family, especially considering how the world was falling apart.

If they lived in a time of peace, maybe that would make things different. But right now, people could die at any moment. There was a darkness to the world that had not been there when Slater was a young boy. People were losing their shine… and it wasn't just the people, either. It was the world itself. The air seemed darker, the plants seemed less vibrant, and many of the shadows appeared to be alive.

They danced in the corner of his vision at night, taunting him. Reminding Slater that there was no way to tell what the world would go through in the coming years. Did Slater really want to stay around and see it for himself? Did he want to know how this wretched story ended?

The thought haunted him day in and day out, weighing him down and serving to stir up his depression. He struggled with the thought of it, the very concept leaving him unsettled and ill.

He didn't want to die. He was afraid of it. Dreadfully afraid of it. And that man that he had seen cackling and falling, having gone mad for whatever reason, only said one thing to him. Not verbally, of course, but it reminded Slater of the paper he had found years ago… it had reminded him of the thing that he feared more than anything else in the world.

Death is terrible, horrible, and only meant for those who didn't deserve to live in this world. I don't want to be undeserving. I want to continuing living. How can I be ready to leave a life when I haven't even fully lived it yet? Slater thought desperately.

One might ask, why was he so desperate? After all, only half of his life had been over, and he still had a good several decades left at best.

He wasn't overweight; he wasn't a slob. Slater had taken care of himself, largely due to his immense knowledge of how the world worked, but also due to his deep-rooted fear of death. It was a striking thing, being afraid of death. It could make you live longer. It might have made Slater live longer too, if not for one thing.

Slater was not a completely healthy man. You see, he also had Lung Cancer.

The people in his family smoked. It's what they did. It was a big part of all of their social gatherings; they would stand out around the grill and share a cigarette. Or they would smoke cigars and indulge in beer and wine whenever they were celebrating an occasion. They were a successful and happy family, and events happened pretty often.

That meant there was a lot of social smoking being done. And even beyond that, Slater smoked during his own time. He took a cigarette break at ten, twelve, and two every single day that he worked, and he had no problem lighting up a cigar in his house to puff on while he watched a movie in the evening, or while he did his crossword puzzle in the morning.

Lung Disease ran in his family because almost everyone behaved the same way. It's where Slater had gotten such a nasty habit. His father had fibrosis in his lungs, and his mother had Pulmonary Lung Disease. And now, it was his turn, and he had the worst of the lot.

Lung Cancer.

The words were like a knife to the heart. Two words, and they managed to bring up every fear that Slater had ever felt and shove it back at him ten-fold. It was a disease that could bring him to his knees. His parents had both been killed by their illnesses, and Slater had done a lot of research into ailments such as this in his youth.

Slater knew his chances of surviving were slim. He knew that death was no longer a distant threat, but one that had broken into his own home and was now holding him at gun point. It was a threat that he had to deal with — not twenty years down the line, but right now, in this very moment.

He tried to run, but death soon caught up to him. Finally. Terribly. Truly.

"It'll be okay, Dad." His son told him, patting him on the shoulder. "It's just cancer. You'll beat it. Don't worry, you're not gonna topple over tomorrow."

He was trying to be encouraging, but it didn't work. This diagnosis had left Slater broken.

That is the only problem, my son. Slater wanted to say, but he couldn't. He was absolutely wrecked. *I never want to topple over. I never want to leave. I want to be here with you always.*

Instead, he tried to be reassuring and simply gave his son a tearful smile, promising to speak with him tomorrow. Slater simply couldn't find the strength to disagree or argue with anyone anymore. He could barely find the strength to say more than a couple words. Slater knew that the cancer would be his ultimate end, and he knew that it would be one that he would face soon.

He could feel it.

The disease was inside of him, eating him alive day and night, making every breath a little more difficult than the last. Now that Slater knew the sickness was in him, he couldn't stop obsessing over the cancer. It felt like the virus was feeding off of him, like the virus was going to rise up and strike him dead at any moment.

And he never stopped looking for an escape. He never stopped looking for a way out. Never stopped looking for a way to escape any possible death that was awaiting him. If there was a new age technique out there, he had tried it. If there was someone who could offer him spiritual services to try and kill the cancer, he had tried it.

Every attempt was a failure, and each failure struck harder than the last. Still, Slater never gave up hope. He was determined that somehow, he would be able to find a cure.

And, eventually, he did find a cure. In the form of pills.

Revolutionary pills that were so impressive, so life-changing, that Slater would've murdered everyone who came between him and the miracle pills. But something like this, it couldn't exist without a cost. Slater was smart. He knew how things like this worked. He knew that they weren't supposed to exist. And yet, here they were, pills that were proven to alter reality so that they could grant a person's greatest wish.

It didn't matter what the wish was, either! Supposedly, these pills were able to make it come true. They were able to make sure that a person could accomplish absolutely anything that they wanted, without having to put forth any undue effort.

They could make you the prettiest woman to ever exist. They could make you the richest man in the world. Why, they could even cure cancer!

Slater knew that a lot of effort probably went behind the pills. A lot of it. But that didn't change the fact that there was a potential way to stop himself from dying, and even more important than that, these pills were a potential way to make sure that his greatest fear would never run its course.

These pills could make him immortal, ensuring that he'd never have to die.

To think, immortality was right there, at the tips of his fingers! Slater was smart. He didn't rush into it. He thought things through, looked things over. Made certain that he understood what it would take to get a hold of these pills.

As more people became aware of the pills, the price on them began to rise. Up and up, first by a few hundred dollars, and then by a few thousand. Finally, they had amassed a truly staggering price tag.

At a price of two million, only the very elite and wealthy were able to obtain one. That was a lot, even for him. His parents did leave him their life-savings, but that was to be divided and shared between him and his siblings, and no way would he ever get their blessing for something that could potentially make him immortal. It went against everything nature intended.

Slater knew that. He knew the theories behind it; he knew the philosophical debates that an act like this could bring about. He had studied everything that he could get his hands on, after all.

The idea of becoming immortal was scorned by nearly everyone.

But he couldn't handle it. The thought of death, right above his head, he couldn't handle it. He didn't want to die by something that he had brought onto himself. It was painful. Not just the cancer itself, but the treatment. The chemotherapy sessions were leaving him dreadfully ill. There were some days where he couldn't even get out of bed because he was so nauseous. His hair had started to fall out in clumps, and his hands shook constantly. He was pale and gaunt. He looked terrible. He felt terrible.

Worst of all?

It wasn't helping.

The chemo didn't seem to be making a lick of difference when it came to the cancer. The illness had grabbed onto Slater hard and didn't seem to want to let go.

So, out of his own savings, out of his own funds, he paid the full price, and after eight long months of waiting, he finally got the pill.

The death-defying pill. A completely golden pill powerful enough to make someone immortal. Only those who had money or those truly desperate were able to get their hands on one. Only those who were mad or insane enough were able to get their hands on the pill. But he didn't care what anyone thought of him. He didn't care if his entire family hated him because of it. He needed the pill.

Did it make him a bad person? Slater didn't think so. It should've been the forefront of everyone's mind, fearing death. It should have been something that people would understand.

Slater didn't want to slowly wither away in a hospital bed, which was where his life was headed. He didn't want to lose everything that he had worked so hard for.

He made up his mind.

With two million dollars saved up, he bought the pill, and he took it home. He sat in his room and stared at it, thinking things over one last time. Slater knew that this was going to change everything, but was that really so bad? Would it really matter if it meant that he was never going to have to succumb to death, that he would be able to meet every member of his family, despite when they were born?

That the cancer would be gone?

He didn't think so.

And so, he took the pill. He let the darkness consume him and stared into the face of the demonic creature, who looked back at him and whispered… something. It wasn't a warning. The words were muddled and made no sense, but Slater thought it might have been a congratulation. It didn't really matter.

Slater didn't care about this strange monstrous being with sharp fangs and thorny skin, who touched his throat and left black marks on his skin. He only cared about the fact that he could feel the cancer cells dying inside of him, one by one.

The very next day, Slater realized something. He no longer needed to gasp to breathe. He no longer needed oxygen, and he no longer felt the tiredness that came with the disease. He was free of it. Free of the disease that had sent him to the path of death. Free of the disease that was causing him to be so desperate, so afraid.

The doctors confirmed it the next day when he went in for a check-up. He had defeated it completely and was in full recovery. Something that could never happened, ever again. But his doctors knew he had done something, taken something.

"You took the pill, didn't you?" the Chief Director of the hospital asked, smiling toothily. She was an elderly woman with graying hair and skin. "That was a stupid decision, and you'll live to regret it, like I am."

Slater found out what she meant a week later, when she was found dead in her office. Apparently, she had passed away from heroin overdose. She had taken the pill to prevent this very thing from happening, but for some reason, it had killed her prematurely instead.

It didn't affect Slater, at first. The death of some woman he had only just met had nothing to do with him. He was immortal. That's all that mattered.

But soon enough, he began to experience the effects of his pill. He was forced to watch all his loved ones pass away, his children, his grandchildren, and even his great-grandchildren, watching in despair as everyone he had ever been close to all started fading away.

"I can't believe you're still here," his great-great-grandson, Alex, said one day. "Mom said you were supposed to die nearly a century ago."

"I know, son. I know. But sometimes, life has a way of surprising us," Slater said, grinning crookedly. He was happy, elated that he could be here for Alex's wedding. "And now you, the first of seven, are getting married. I don't even know what to say. Out of everyone, I never expected you to get married first."

"Well… time changes people." Alex smiled at him. "And it changed me, too. But you? Time hasn't changed you at all! I mean, look at you! You look like you haven't aged a day!"

Slater blinked and tilted his head. He looked at the mirror that Alex was standing in front of, and he walked closer to it, narrowing his eyes. His eyes widened as he noticed what Alex was pointing at. Slater had all the facial features he had when he was still a mere human. The mole that had erupted on the right side of his nose, his scruffy beard, his bushy eyebrows, everything. He actually realized something else as well.

He had not shaved once since he took the pill. He didn't need to. Nor did he need to cut his hair or fingernails. It was as if things just suddenly stopped.

He was stuck in time. He was literally stuck in time, not ageing a single day for the past century. And the words that the elderly doctor had said to him hit him like a bullet train.

"You took the pill, didn't you? You made a mistake, Slater, a mistake that you are bitterly going to regret. Just like I am."

And with that, he began to realize. That he really wasn't going to die. That he would be stuck in this world forever. He had no idea where to go from here, what to do. For the greed, the obsession of completing one's own dream, and the lack of care for others, had already destroyed half the world. He would have seen it if it wasn't for his rose-tinted glasses, but he didn't know…

Exactly what the darkness and despair of the pills were doing to the world. And by the time he realized… it had been too late.

Seven Deadly Sins

Seven Deadly Sins